# THE INVISIBLE ASSASSIN

## THE MALICHEA QUEST

# THE INVISIBLE ASSASSIN

## THE MALICHEA QUEST

# JIM ELDRIDGE

**BLOOMSBURY**

LONDON  BERLIN  NEW YORK  SYDNEY

Bloomsbury Publishing, London, Berlin, New York and Sydney

First published in Great Britain in April 2012 by Bloomsbury
Publishing Plc 50 Bedford Square, London, WC1B 3DP

A CIP catalogue record for this book is available from the British Library

ISBN 978 1 4088 1719 3

Typeset by Hewer Text UK Ltd, Edinburgh
Printed in Great Britain by Clays Ltd, St Ives Plc, Bungay, Suffolk

1 3 5 7 9 10 8 6 4 2

www.bloomsbury.com

*To Lynne, the inspiration for this hidden library*

# Chapter 1

The building site was much like any other, except for the small band of protestors standing outside the fence holding handmade placards that read 'STOP IT' and 'SACRED PLACE'. Jake Wells, a trainee press officer (or 'spin doctor', as he preferred to think of it) for the Department of Science reflected that, as protests went, it was pretty feeble. Five people and a small unkempt dog. Hardly up there with a mass student demo in the centre of London. Still, it was a protest, and as they were protesting against the construction of a new university science block on what they claimed was the site of a fairy ring, it came under his remit.

A fairy ring, for heaven's sake! He guessed that's why he'd been given this particular job. This was a story that most of the others in the press office wouldn't touch with a bargepole. But Jake wasn't like the others. It seemed that everyone else in his department had come through the same route: public school, then university, mostly Oxford or Cambridge. When a national newspaper had pointed out how elitist this was, the department had acted to prove them wrong: a competition had been launched to offer an opportunity for a trainee press officer from what was called 'the disadvantaged'. Jake had entered. He fitted the bill perfectly: abandoned at birth, brought up in an orphanage and then a string of foster homes, and he had left school at sixteen because he couldn't afford to go on to further education. After he left school, he worked in a series of dead-end jobs. But always he had one burning ambition: to be a journalist. Every spare moment he had, he practised writing witty and biting articles about the issues of the day, exposing corrupt politicians. But getting into journalism wasn't that easy: he discovered that he needed a degree.

It was while he had been wondering how to get over this problem that he'd read about the Department of Science competition, entered it, and won his place. At last, his big oppportunity! At eighteen years of age, he'd made it! Not quite the journalism he had dreamed of, but a proper job where he could hone his writing skills.

That had been nine months ago, and after nine months he was still a trainee press officer. The problem was, as Jake saw it, they didn't know what to do with him. He wasn't 'one of them'; he didn't have the same Oxbridge connections, or relatives inside other government departments, so they didn't want to give him anything too 'sensitive'. Something where he could upset important people. So, instead, he was given the soft stories, the quirky ones. Like this one: the threat to a fairy ring.

But if I do a really good job on this one, quell the protest and come out of it smelling of roses, maybe they'll see I can actually *do* this job, Jake kept saying to himself, and next time I'll get a proper assignment. Maybe something controversial, like climate change. That was always a sure-fire step up the promotion ladder.

As he looked at the scene before him, Jake noticed that there weren't any TV cameras, or even local radio. Just a local journalist from the *Bedfordshire Times* who'd arranged to meet Jake at the site of the protest. Jake thought he saw her now: a woman in her mid-twenties talking to the protestors and jotting down notes on a pad.

Jake headed for the small group. Inside the fence, all was noise: heavy machinery, diggers tearing up the ground for the foundations for the new science block.

The young woman was talking to the elderly woman

holding the placard saying 'Sacred place', and Jake heard her asking the woman her age, identifying her at once as a journalist. What was the local print media's obsession with age? he thought. Every story had to have people's ages in brackets. 'Local businesswoman, Pauline Stone (37) . . .' or 'Mad serial killer, Victor Nutter (63) . . .'

'Penny Johnson?' he asked, and the young woman turned to face him, nodding. Jake smiled, his best press officer's smile. 'Jake Wells, Department of Science. We spoke on the phone.'

Before the young journalist could respond, the elderly woman brandished her placard at Jake angrily.

'You should be ashamed of yourself!' she shouted. 'This is a sacred place. Fairies have lived at this spot untroubled by humankind for thousands of years!'

'And I'm sure they can continue to live here,' said Jake, putting on what he hoped was a sincere expression. He struggled to remember the argument he'd been told to propose to the protestors by one of his senior colleagues. It had seemed pretty unbelievable, but it was the party line, and if he wanted to get on . . . 'As I understand it, fairies are other-dimensional, and the study of other-dimensional states of existence will be one of the areas being looked at by the new science department . . .'

'Don't you patronise me, young man!' shouted the woman. 'No good will come of this! He who disturbs this land is cursed!'

The other four protestors nodded in agreement, and the dog, held on a rather loose leash by one of them, growled at Jake. Jake, who was never fond of dogs at the best of times, especially small snappy ones, forced a smile. This wasn't going well.

'I'm sorry you feel like that,' he said. 'And the department is doing its best to minimise the disturbance to the site . . .'

'Minimise!' echoed the woman, incredulously. 'Minimise!!' She pointed her placard towards the building site, and Jake and the young journalist turned to see a huge JCB dig its bucket deep into the soil and rip it up. 'Do you seriously call that minimal disturbance?!'

'Well,' began Jake, forcing himself to keep his smile in place, 'I do agree that it *looks* as if there is a lot of damage being done, but a building can't just be put up overnight . . .'

*Whack!* The woman swung her placard and hit Jake over the head with it.

'Ow!' said Jake. 'Now look . . . !'

*Whack!* The placard swung once more, and again he felt the impact, but this time he managed to get his arm up to protect his head.

'There's no need for violence!' he protested.

'Oh yes there is!' said the elderly woman. 'This sacred piece of land is being violated by you and your lot!'

Jake realised that she was drawing the placard back for another bash at him, and that the leash holding the growling dog seemed to have loosened further.

'I'll go and have a word with the diggers,' he offered hastily.

With that he moved nimbly away and headed for the fence and the diggers. He was aware that the reporter, Penny Johnson, was by his side.

'I suppose being attacked is an occupational hazard for you,' she said. 'After all, you are part of a very unpopular government.'

'I'm not part of the government,' said Jake. 'I just work for them as a press officer.'

'You defend them,' said Johnson.

'I would never defend them if I thought they were wrong,' insisted Jake. Inwardly, he reflected that he was glad this wasn't *Pinocchio*, or his nose would be growing longer.

Most of his job so far seemed to consist of defending the government's taking yet another wrong decision.

They had reached the fence now, and the wooden security hut by the entrance gate. Jake took out his ID card and held it open for the security guard on duty to examine. He gestured at Johnson and said, 'She's with me.'

'Where are your hard hats?' asked the security guard.

Damn! thought Jake. I knew there was something I'd forgotten. 'I didn't realise we needed them at this stage of construction,' he said. 'After all, they're just digging for the foundations.'

'No hard hats, no entry,' said the security guard. 'Those are my orders.'

Out of the corner of his eye, Jake spotted a couple of hard hats lying just inside the hut.

'We'll borrow those two,' he said, pointing.

The security guard frowned, then shook his head.

'Those belong to the company,' he said. 'Company use only.'

Johnson began scribbling something in her notebook. Jake could guess what it was, something along the lines of 'Red faces at protest. A top government official was refused entry to the site where the controversial new university science block is under construction . . . blah blah blah'. Not that he was a 'top government official', but it sounded better than 'trainee press officer'. Jake realised if he wasn't to come out of this looking like a complete idiot, he had to do something, exert what little authority he had on this situation before he lost control of it completely. It was time for a bluff. Once again, Jake took out his ID card and held it out to the security guard.

'If you read this card properly, you will see that I am representing the government minister responsible for this particular project,' he said firmly. 'My orders are to make an inspection today and report back. Now, if you refuse to loan us the use of those two hard hats and let us into this site, I shall telephone my department head and have this whole site closed down immediately, until such time as authority is given to supply us with the necessary hard hats. That will cost the company many hundreds of thousands of pounds and will also prejudice other contracts they have on tender with my department.'

Before the security guard could respond, Jake took out his mobile phone, poised his finger over the dial button, and continued smoothly but firmly: 'Or perhaps you'd prefer to talk to the minister yourself, and explain to him why the site is being closed down, and he can then explain that to your boss.' Jake nearly added, 'So what's it be? Come on, punk, make my day,' but refrained. As it was he was trembling inside, terrified that the security guard would call his bluff and make him look even more of an idiot.

The security guard hesitated, then scowled and reached inside the hut. He produced the two hard hats, which Jake and Johnson put on. The inside of Jake's stank of grease, and part of him regretted insisting on being given it, but it was too late to back down now.

'Thank you,' he said.

Then he and Johnson walked through the gateway and on to the site.

'Very macho.' Johnson grinned. 'I thought you said you weren't part of the government?'

'Hmmm,' said Jake non-commitally, and kept on walking, repeating to himself the mantra the senior press officer had driven into him on his first day: be careful about any comments you make when reporters are around.

The site was alive with activity and noise: huge yellow machines digging, dumper trucks running to and fro laden with dirt and rubble. If there were any fairies here, they'll be long gone, thought Jake.

A shout above the noise of the machines caught his attention. It came from a hole not far away. Jake headed towards the hole, Johnson tagging along just behind him, notebook and pen at the ready. A huge digger was poised at the edge of the hole, and the driver had withdrawn the equally huge claw-like bucket to the rim. One of the building workers had jumped down into the hole and was scrabbling with his hands at something half-buried in the earth.

Oh, please, God, don't let it be a body! groaned Jake inwardly, especially with a reporter at the scene.

But no, it appeared to be a parcel of some sort, wrapped in what looked to Jake from this distance like some kind of oiled leather.

Don't let it be a head, prayed Jake silently. Not even a head from ancient times!

Television news loved pictures of skulls being dug out of the ground. And the bunch of loonies with their placards outside the fence would love it as well; they'd claim it was the head of a fairy king, or some such nonsense. Jake reflected that it was lucky there were no TV cameras here, after all.

But it wasn't a head. The building worker stood in the hole started to unwrap the worn leather casing, and revealed what looked like some sort of big old book. He began to open it.

Jake heard a gasp of alarm from Johnson.

'Shouldn't you stop them?' she asked. 'That could be really ancient. He might damage it.'

'Yes.' Jake nodded. 'I was just about to do that.' Aloud, he called to the worker in the hole, 'Hey! You shouldn't have opened that!'

The man glared up at Jake.

'Why not?' he said.

'Because . . .' began Jake. And then he faltered. Why not? He was sure there was some Act of Parliament or other preventing it, but he couldn't remember what it was. It was something to do with the Queen. 'Because

'. . . all property found on this land is the property of the Queen, and as the representative of Her Majesty's Government on this site . . .'

Jake never finished. The building worker's expression suddenly changed from one of contempt to one of fear as he dropped the boook, and then he was shaking his arm as if trying to throw off a creature, like a spider or something.

And then Jake saw the man's hand began to change, turning from a skin colour to a faint green, and the green began to blossom out, like a plant sprouting leaves at rapid speed, but these weren't leaves, they were . . . fungus. A kind of green fungus was enveloping the whole of the man's arm, creeping upwards, spreading out.

As Jake and the others watched in horror, the man ran for the edge of the hole, trying to scramble up the sides, but whatever he was trying to escape from had already got hold of him. Before their eyes, the green fungus spread, covering the man's chest, spreading rapidly downwards over his thighs, his legs, and upwards to his neck, and his head. The man was screaming in fear, but then his screams were cut off; he had disappeared and been replaced by a mass of writhing green fungus.

The weird shape tried to move, to the left, to the right, struggling, and then it collapsed. The next second

11

everyone was yelling and running away from the scene, desperate to put distance between themselves and the mass of what had once been a human being.

Everyone except Jake, who was rooted to the spot in spite of himself, just staring, goggle-eyed, at what was happening.

# Chapter 2

'He turned into a vegetable right in front of me!'

It was the next morning and Jake was back in his office at Whitehall, relating the astonishing events of the afternoon before to his colleague Paul Evans. Paul was two years older than Jake and had been at the department for over a year, which made him an old press hand in Jake's eyes.

'What sort of vegetable?' asked Paul.

'What does it matter what sort of vegetable?!' exploded Jake. 'It was . . . it was . . .' He shook his head. 'Unbelievable! Like something out of a horror movie!'

'What did you do?' asked Paul.

'I did what I've been told to do: slapped a D Notice on the whole thing, which meant the reporter who was there . . . and luckily for me the *only* reporter who was there, and a local at that – if it had been one of

13

the nationals I'd have been well and truly sunk . . . anyway, which meant the reporter was stopped from telling anyone what had happened. And then I got on the phone to Gareth. Within twenty minutes, the site was full of helicopters landing, the SAS turning up fully armed, medics, and of course the top brass from the press office to make sure the whole place was shut down. By the time I left, there was a net of security around the site like I've never seen. Everyone in the area was taken in and had the fear of God put into them, and was persuaded they'd been the unfortunate victims of a hallucination caused by a leak of toxic gas.'

'Maybe it was,' said Paul. 'Maybe there was a leak of toxic gas, some substance buried long ago. Some experiment that went wrong during the First World War, or something. There's all manner of terrible stuff buried all over the place.'

'I know what I saw!' insisted Jake.

'You know what you *think* you saw,' countered Paul. 'That's what happens with hallucinations.' He gave Jake a grin. 'Considering everything, you did well, Jake, for a trainee.'

But it *wasn't* a hallucination. Jake knew what he'd seen. A man had picked up something wrapped in faded leather. He'd unwrapped it and exposed an old book.

When he'd opened it, a fungus had started to spread up his arm, and within seconds it had covered his whole body. He remembered an ambulance turning up, and paramedics in complete body-protection suits putting that . . . thing . . . on a stretcher and taking it to the ambulance, and then speeding away. No siren sounding, so he guessed the man was dead. The site itself was sealed off, with armed guards posted around it, all dressed in radiation protection suits, just in case there was still something dangerous there. So how could it have been a hallucination?

'News about it is bound to leak out,' said Jake. 'D Notice or not, one of those workers, or one of the protestors, is going to phone up their local TV station.'

'What protestors?' asked Paul.

'These people who were protesting against building a new science block on the site. They said it was the home of fairies and mustn't be disturbed.'

'Fairies?' chuckled Paul.

'Don't laugh.' Jake shuddered. 'One woman said to me if the ground was disturbed then whoever did it was cursed. And look what happened!'

'Nothing happened,' insisted Paul. 'Like they said, mass hallucination.'

'It wasn't,' insisted Jake. 'I saw it. They saw it. And at least one of them will tell what happened, and some news editor hungry for an interesting item for page two will write it up.'

Paul shook his head.

15

'It'll soon get squashed,' he said. 'H or H.'

Jake frowned.

'What?'

'H or H,' repeated Paul. 'Hoax or Hallucination. The standard rebuttal to any story of that kind, whether it's UFOs, people vanishing into thin air, weird monsters, spontaneous combustion, anything out of the ordinary. I'm surprised you weren't told about H or H.' Paul shrugged. 'But then, you've only been here . . . what?'

'I've been here nine months!' protested Jake.

'But you haven't had to deal with one of these stories so far. So, now you have. Welcome to the wonderful world of H or H.'

Jake was about to carry on his protest about what he'd seen, when his phone rang.

'Jake Wells,' he said.

It was Gareth Findlay-Weston, his head of section in the press office.

'Jake,' said Gareth. Even though Jake couldn't see Gareth, he could tell by the tone of his voice Gareth was smiling. Or, at least, that he had a smile on his face, which wasn't necessarily the same thing. 'Can you pop up to my office?'

Gareth's office was on the third floor. Jake and Paul and the rest of the grunts in the press office were on the first floor. As Jake walked up the stairs he reflected on how the floor levels indicated seniority. In fact, the whole building that was the Department of Science reflected levels of seniority. The higher you went, the more intimidating the building became: the banisters changed from ordinary metal to brass. The light fittings, which were plain white plastic up to the second floor, became shining gunmetal from the third floor upwards. Jake wondered what the fittings were made of when you got beyond the fourth floor: solid gold, perhaps, or maybe platinum.

He walked along the narrow corridor, panelled with dark oak, the wood adorned with old paintings showing an England long past: hunting scenes, old countryside celebrations, all of it looking backwards. It hardly went with the image the Department of Science liked to present, as thrusting boldly into the twenty-first century. Though the public would never come this far, never see these pictures or the dark oak panels. They'd be kept at the lower levels, the second floor and below, where it was all chromium lighting, modern prints and small abstract shapes, models of molecular structures and large plasma screens.

Jake arrived at Gareth's door, knocked, and went in to be met by Gareth's assistant, Janet.

'He's ready for you,' said Janet, ushering Jake smartly over to an inner office.

Gareth was sitting behind a huge desk that wouldn't have looked out of place in a James Bond film. There was very little on the desk, except two telephones and a photograph in a silver frame showing his wife and sons.

'Jake!' Gareth greeted him, the usual broad smile. He waved him to a chair. 'Well done, Jake. Damn good stuff yesterday! For a trainee, you did a magnificent job under difficult circumstances. You did absolutely the right thing, getting on to me. Averted what could have been a mass panic.'

'What about the man?'

'Which man?'

'The building worker. The one who . . . you know . . . turned into that thing.'

Gareth frowned.

'Are you feeling all right, Jake?' he asked.

'Yes,' said Jake. 'Obviously a bit shaken up. I mean, it's not every day you see something like that . . .'

Gareth got up from his chair and came round the desk to Jake, a look of concern on his face.

'Did you get yourself checked?' he asked. 'By the medicos, I mean.'

'Well . . . no,' said Jake. 'If you remember, you ordered me to come back here to deal with the press because you sent Algy to take over control of the press at the site. You said the situation called for someone with more experience.'

Gareth shook his head apologetically.

'I'm dreadfully sorry, Jake. I was terribly lax. Trying to stop it turning into a media circus. I think you'd better go and see the quack and get yourself checked out.'

'But the man who tuned into that . . . thing,' insisted Jake.

Gareth gave Jake a hard look.

'It didn't happen,' he said firmly. 'There was some sort of leak of toxic gas which gave everyone the heebie-jeebies and made them see things.' Then his expression softened. 'I'm sorry, Jake. After all, as your immediate boss I have a duty of care to you and everyone in my department. So, go to the medico department and get yourself checked out. It could be you've still got traces of the gas, whatever it was, in your system. Get fixed up now. Then we'll talk afterwards.'

Gareth gave a smile and patted Jake on the shoulder, then he picked up his internal phone and tapped out a number.

'Infirmary,' he said, 'Findlay-Weston. One of my department needs a check-up as a result of this gas leak that happened in Bedfordshire. Yes, he's still suffering the after-effects, so I'm sending him along to you. His name's Jake Wells. Give him a full once-over, and any treatment he needs. Bill my department. Quote my name as reference.'

\* \* \*

19

Fifteen minutes later, a semi-naked Jake was in the basement of the building, being prodded and poked by a doctor in a white coat while a nurse stood by and made notes. It was a thorough examination, no doubt about that. Blood pressure. Blood sample. Urine sample. Weight. A lung test, blowing into a funnel connected to some machine. Eyes tested, lights shone into them; followed by a standard optician's eye test.

At the end of it, when Jake had dressed, the doctor handed him a prescription.

'You'll need to take these three times a day,' he said.

'Why?' asked Jake. 'What's wrong with me?'

'We're not sure,' said the doctor. 'You've apparently been exposed to some kind of toxic gas, but there's no indication of what sort of gas it is, what the constituents are. All we know are the symptoms, a kind of hallucination.'

It was on the tip of Jake's tongue to say, 'It wasn't a hallucination! I saw a man turn into some kind of heaving mass of vegetation!' but he decided against it. It might make the doctor send him for psychiatric reports, and who knew what that might unleash?

Jake took the prescription.

'So, what are these things?'

'They're anti-hallucinogens,' said the doctor. 'You should be back to normal in a day or so, once they've cleared through your system.' He scribbled on another piece of paper, tore it off a pad, and handed it to Jake. 'This is a sick certificate for twenty-four hours. Come back and see me on Thursday and we'll check you over again. Make an appointment with the nurse on your way out.'

As Jake left the room, he was sure of one thing: he wasn't going to be taking the pills. What he'd seen hadn't been a hallucination.

# Chapter 3

Ten minutes later, Jake was back in Gareth's office, showing him the sick note and the prescription. This time Gareth didn't smile. Instead he sighed heavily and sympathetically.

'My poor Jake,' he said. 'It looks like you've become a victim of this tragedy.' Then the sigh switched back to a reassuring smile again as he added, 'But only temporarily, if the medico's right. And there's no reason to think he isn't. After all, this is the Department of Science, and if we can't have the best that modern medicine has to offer in this country, then who can?'

Taking Jake's arm and steering him towards the outer office and Janet, Gareth continued, 'Twenty-four hours, then I'm sure everything'll be fine. And don't worry about work. I've detailed Paul Evans to take care of your stuff until you get back. The main thing is: rest and recovery.' Gareth opened his door and patted Jake on the back in a blokey sort of way. 'You're a good man, Jake, with a future here. You've already shown that with the way you handled this situation. We need you, and we need you in good form. Look after yourself.'

Jake trudged down the marble stairs with their brass handrails, crossing the boundary to stairs with metal handrails, and back to the big open-plan office. Paul was sitting at his desk, on the phone, which he hung up as Jake returned.

'I've got the news,' he said. 'Janet phoned me. You've got tomorrow off and I've got your workload.' He grinned. 'Lucky beggar. Maybe I ought to pretend to be seeing things and get a day off.'

Jake shrugged and forced a grin. 'It worked for me,' he said.

He saw that Paul had already added Jake's most recent files to his own pile of work in his pending file. On the top was a fresh folder marked 'Bedfordshire Incident'.

'Things have moved fast,' said Jake, pointing to the file.

Paul nodded.

'Remember the first rule: being in the press office means being one step ahead,' he said. 'The modern media work by split seconds, not hours. Something happens in the UK, within seconds the rest of the world knows about it.'

Jake flicked opened the file. Inside was his own report on the incident, along with a list of names and addresses: the people who'd been there: building contractors, protestors, Penny Johnson, the paramedics who'd attended, even the SAS men who'd arrived, although they were only identified as 'Soldier A' and 'Soldier B', and so on. Halfway down the second page, where there was the description of the man 'apparently becoming infected' (the phrase was in inverted commas and the letters 'H or H' next to it), someone had written the word 'SIGMA' in capitals.

'What's this mean?' asked Jake. 'Sigma?'

Paul looked.

'Ah yes, I've seen that before,' he said. 'Gareth's writing. I think it's a kind of shorthand for H or H.'

'Hardly shorthand,' said Jake. 'It would take longer to write.'

Paul shrugged. 'You know these Oxford types. They like to use phrases that sound classical. Have you noticed the amount of Latin they use when they talk to one another. A bit pretentious, if you ask me.'

Paul was a Cambridge man.

'Possibly.' Jake nodded.

'So,' Paul grinned, 'that's you off. What will you do?'

'Rest and recover,' said Jake. 'Those are my orders from upstairs, and I mean to obey them to the letter.'

He headed to his own desk. 'I just need to sort out a couple of things, and then I'm off.'

'No need,' said Paul. 'Janet was most insistent that you just pack up and go now. Gareth's orders. She said he's worried about you.'

'That's very flattering,' said Jake. Then Paul's phone rang.

'Evans, press office,' he said briskly, and whatever the query was immediately grabbed his full attention, so Jake was able to get back to his desk without further arguments.

Beneath his apparent happiness at getting two days off on full pay, Jake was puzzled. It was all too easy. Was it really concern about his health? And he *had* seen what he'd seen at that building site, he was sure of it. But had that really been a hallucination, as Gareth and the doctor suggested? And was this feeling that something wasn't right an extension of that, a linked form of paranoia?

Jake sat down at his computer. He was about to switch it off, when something made him go to the department's internal search engine and type in 'Sigma'. Immediately, the message came up: 'Restricted to Level 4 or above.' Jake's security clearance was Level 2. Receptionists were Level 1. Trainee and junior press officers were Level 2. Cleaning staff were Level 3.

Jake closed down his computer, picked up his briefcase, then waved goodbye to Paul as he headed for the

25

door. Paul was still on the phone and gave him a wave and a thumbs-up back.

Jake knew it would be the wisest thing to just leave the building and go home. Watch a DVD or two. Eat pizza. Take a walk. Do a gallery. But instead he went down to the basement level of the building, to the archives. He showed his pass to the security guard on duty, and then went to the central desk marked 'Information'. Two librarians were there. One was busy at her computer terminal, too busy to take notice of Jake. The other, a middle-aged man, smiled at him.

'Yes?' he asked. 'Can I help you?'

Jake proffered his pass to the man.

'Jake Wells, press office,' he said. 'I'm looking to see if you've got anything on Sigma.'

'Sigma?'

Jake spelt it for him, and the man typed it in. There was a pause, then the man gave a rueful smile.

'I'm sorry, Mr Wells, the Sigma files are for Level Four and above only, and as you know, your pass is only Level Two. I'm sure if you talk to your department head, he or she will be able to access whatever information you want.'

Jake was hitting a brick wall. He forced a smile.

'I understand,' he said. 'I'll do that.'

He half turned to go, and then turned back to the librarian again.

'Oh, one more thing,' he said. 'A different question this time. I had a call from a local paper, the *Bedfordshire Times*. A reporter called Penny Johnson. Do you have a file on her?'

'I'll check.'

Once again the librarian typed a few words in, and this time he nodded.

'Yes, there is a file,' he said. He pressed a key on his keyboard, and a small piece of paper rolled off the printer on the desk. The librarian tore it off and handed it to Jake.

'Take that to the search desk and they'll hand you the file. But remember, you are not allowed to remove it.'

'I understand.' Jake nodded. 'Thank you.'

He went to the search desk at the other side of the archive library and handed in the slip of paper. The search desk librarian disappeared, then reappeared a few moments later with a slim file marked 'P. Johnson'. Once again, Jake was instructed that he couldn't remove the file from the archive library, and he nodded and took it to one of the tables.

There was a lot of information about Penelope Barbara Johnson. Her age, her address, her parents, her schools (even including her pre-school), where she'd studied journalism on a media studies course. Jake made a note of her phone numbers, both at home

27

and at the office of the *Bedfordshire Times*. There was no note of her mobile phone number. The very last page was the most recent: the incident the previous day at the building site. The details were those written by Jake, detailing the protest at the site, and the transformation of the building worker into a hideous form, with additional material from Algernon Ainsworth about the mass hallucination caused by the leak of toxic gas.

So Algy has put the official spin on it, mused Jake. He turned over the page and saw on the back that someone had written in pencil, *Sigma – poss Malichea?*

What did 'Malichea' mean?

Jake returned the file to the search desk, thanked the assistant, then went back to the information desk and the librarian.

'Sorry to keep troubling you,' he said with a smile, 'but there is one last thing I need to check on. Have you got anything on Malichea?'

'How do you spell that?' asked the librarian.

Jake spelt it out and the librarian typed it in, and then gave Jake an apologetic smile. 'I'm sorry, that information is also restricted to Level Four and above. You'll need to talk to your department head.'

'I will.' Jake smiled. 'Thanks anyway.'

'Jake!'

A familiar voice behind him made him turn. It was Gareth.

'Jake, still here? I thought you'd be at home by now.'

Jake gave an apologetic smile.

'There were just a couple of things I wanted to check . . .'

Gareth chuckled.

'Be careful, Jake, or you'll be turning into a work-aholic. Believe me, it's not a good thing to be. You never see your kids, your wife thinks you're having an affair because you're never at home . . .'

'I'm not married,' said Jake.

'And being a workaholic means you're never likely to be,' said Gareth.

He gave Jake a sympathetic squeeze on the shoulder, the second that day. It struck Jake that Gareth had never done such a thing to him before, touching him like this. Was it some kind of secret Freemason sign, perhaps? Or maybe Gareth was gay and this was his way of hitting on Jake?

'Go on,' said Gareth. 'Go home, Jake. Get some rest and recover. You've had an ordeal. Come back Thursday, see the medico and get yourself cleared as fit, and then you can throw yourself back among the files. We need you, Jake, but we need you fit. No work for the next twenty-four hours. And that's an order.'

29

# Chapter 4

Jake stood on the platform at Victoria underground waiting for the train. The platform was packed with people. Where do they all come from, he thought. At rush hour, he could understand, but this was supposed to be the quiet part of the day. He heard the approaching sound of the train. Automatically, he edged forward, eager to be one of the first on the train and so get a seat. He hated standing, his nose pushed into someone's else's smelly armpits, but it nearly always happened.

The train was nearly out of the tunnel when Jake felt a push in the small of his back. Someone trying to shove in! Jake pressed back, but then was shocked to feel the pressure on his back was firmer, harder, moving him firmly towards the very edge of the platform, shoving hard. If he hadn't already been resisting he'd have been pushed forward on to the lines, right in front of the train.

Jake turned, trying to see who was behind him, and as he did so the person gave one last hard push and he felt himself stumbling and falling, into the path of the oncoming train!

'Look out!'

A man grabbed him and pulled him back, just as the train surged past him. Jake even felt the moving train hit him on the arm. Then he was stumbling back, the man who'd saved him holding his arm.

'You all right, mate?' asked the man, concerned.

Jake studied him. The expression of concern on his face looked genuine.

'Yes.' Jake nodded, still shocked.

The man released his hold on Jake's arm.

'You ought to be more careful, mate,' said the man. 'Losing your balance like that. If I hadn't caught you, you'd have been under that train.'

Jake was about to say, 'I didn't lose my balance. Someone pushed me.' But then he thought how stupid it would sound. Instead, he nodded and thanked the man, and got into the carriage. He found a seat and collapsed into it, still feeling shocked.

Someone had pushed him! Not just once, like an accident, but firmly. A hard push.

Or maybe Gareth was right. Maybe there really had been something toxic in the air at the dig, something

31

that was making him feel paranoid. Why would anyone want to shove him under a train?

All the way to his home station at Finsbury Park Jake thought about what had happened. Had he really been pushed? Even if he had, maybe it hadn't been aimed at him particularly. Maybe it had just been some lunatic who felt like pushing someone under a train for no reason. There were plenty of lunatics at loose in London, some dangerous, some who just sat in parks and talked to themselves.

As the train neared Finsbury Park, his mind turned back to what had happened at the dig, and then at the department afterwards. The words 'Sigma' and 'Malichea' hung in his mind. What were they references to? Something to do with what had happened at the dig, he was sure. But what had happened? He'd seen a man find something wrapped in leather, and open it up to reveal a book. He'd opened the book and then been turned into some kind of mass of vegetation. It sounded like a sci-fi or horror film plot, or something to do with a sort of weird unusual science thing.

As he thought the words 'weird unusual science thing', his mind automatically went to Lauren, his former girlfriend, of very recent and painful times. He suspected he'd deliberately dredged up the phrase about 'weird science' just so he could think of her. Not that he needed any excuse, he often thought of her. Too often. It was a pity she obviously never thought of him these days.

How long had it been since he'd last spoken to her? Three months? And the conversation they'd had then could hardly have been called 'speaking'. She'd hung up on him. And that had been that. Maybe he was just using this as an excuse to talk to her again. Try and start things up again, maybe. Fat chance, he admitted to himself. But then, stranger things had happened. *Were* happening.

As he called up her number, he felt a thrill of anticipation. He heard the call tone, then her voice, still sending a shudder through him the same as always, even with that one brief word:

'Yes?'

Doing his very best to keep his voice calm and relaxed, he said, 'Hi, Lauren. It's Jake.'

'I know,' she said. 'I saw your name.'

Was that a good thing? he wondered. She still had his number saved. But then, from the cold tone in her voice, maybe it wasn't a good thing after all.

He was about to press on, when she said, 'You've got a nerve, calling me. After what you did.'

His heart sank. She hadn't forgotten how he'd hurt her. OK, what he'd done was unforgivable, the sort of thing people don't forget. But he'd hoped time might have helped her forgive him . . . even just a little bit. From the hurt tone of her voice, forgiveness was still a long way off. He took a deep breath, then said, 'Lauren, this isn't about *us* . . .'

'Of course it's about us. You're calling me, aren't you?'

'Yes, but not about us. It's about some weird science thing . . .'

Even as he said it he knew it was the wrong word.

'Weird?'

Her tone on that one was definitely hostile.

'Sorry, not weird. Unorthodox. Unconventional. Look, can I see you? I need to talk about this. I promise not to . . . well . . . start anything.'

Again, he mentally kicked himself for sounding like some desperate love-sick twelve-year-old. Pull yourself together, for heaven's sake! he told himself sharply. 'Lauren, something odd's happening.' His tone was firmer now, more self-assured. A concerned tone, sincere, the tone he used on his job as trainee press officer in order to invoke confidence, no matter how big a lie he was spinning. 'You're the only one I can think of who might be able to throw some light on it.'

There was a pause, then she said, 'OK. I've got a lecture at eleven, then nothing after twelve thirty.

Let's meet somewhere neutral. In the square in front of the British Library. One o'clock.'

'One o'clock,' he agreed. 'I'll see you there.'

As he hung up, he realised he was smiling. He was going to see Lauren again. OK, it wasn't a date. In fact, it wasn't really anything except her agreeing to see him to answer some questions about science. It was the sort of thing she might do for anyone, but, considering what had happened between them at the end, she had agreed to see him. It was a start.

In a large and expensive-looking office on the thirtieth floor of a hi-tech building overlooking the Thames, a phone rang. The man in the office picked it up.

'Yes?' he said.

'We've got an intercept,' said a voice. 'The target has made contact, cell phone to cell phone.

'Who did he call?'

'A Lauren Graham. She's in her second year of a degree in Theoretical Sciences at the University of London. They're meeting in the square in front of the British Library in Euston Road at thirteen hundred hours.'

'OK,' said the man. 'Set the dogs on them.'

# Chapter 5

One o'clock found Jake sitting at a metal table with a cup of coffee in the precinct in front of the British Library, scanning the people as they came in. He wondered if Lauren would be on time. She always had been punctual; he was the one who was usually late. But today, he wanted to show her he'd changed. He was on time.

What had happened had been so stupid. *He'd* been so stupid.

They'd met soon after he'd landed the trainee press officer's job at the Department of Science. He'd been taken to the University of London by an older press officer to show him the ropes, and to talk to some of the students about their work. It was for an article about 'Scientists of the Future'. The facts and figures Jake had been presented with on that day had been overwhelming, and mind-numbing; but one person had stood out among all the others, a first-year student called Lauren Graham. Jake had stopped listening to what she was saying about something called Theoretical Sciences after a minute and had lost himself in her beautiful blue eyes. To his surprise, she seemed quite interested in him, especially once she'd found out that he hadn't come from a university background. The fact that both had no memory of their parents was another bond.

Lauren's parents had been killed soon after she was born, and she'd been brought up by her paternal grandparents, both of who were now dead. At the end of that day, Jake asked her out; and she said yes.

For six months they'd gone out together, getting closer and closer. So close that Jake had been on the point of asking her about moving in with him. And then there had been The Wedding. A friend of Lauren's was getting married, and he and Lauren had gone to the ceremony and the reception. It had seemed to Jake that Lauren was spending an awful lot of time talking to some rugby-playing bloke she knew. Too much time. Smiling at him, laughing, touching his arm, even flicking her fingers through his hair as she pretended to examine his scalp for nits. Robert, that had been his name. Robert the rugby player. And Jake had got fed up with it. And he did the unforgivable. He went off and found one of the bridesmaids, who'd already given him the eye earlier during the ceremony, and he'd got off with her in the bushes behind the drinks tent. Where Lauren had discovered them when she'd come looking for him.

He shuddered even now as he thought about it. He'd tried blaming an excess of drink, but it hadn't washed. It hadn't deserved to. In that one stupid act he'd finished them.

He'd tried to talk to her since, but she'd just hung up on him. He'd tried hanging around places he knew she went, but she had successfully avoided him, her friends had seen to that. The same when he'd tried calling on her at the university. Each time he'd received very firm instructions that 'Ms Graham does not wish to see you'.

And Robert the rugby player had called at Jake's flat one day and warned him that if he didn't lay off, then he, Robert, would make sure that Jake would be in no state to carry on chasing Lauren this way. Jake took the hint.

Six weeks ago, he'd sent her a birthday card to mark her nineteenth birthday, and written 'Sorry' inside the card, but she hadn't replied.

He sipped at his coffee and checked his watch. Five past one. She wasn't coming. She was paying him back. She was standing him up.

And then he saw her, entering the precinct, looking around for him. Seeing her, her long coat swirling around her legs, her slim briefcase held under one arm, her long dark hair framing her face, he felt a pain inside and he wanted to rush to her and grab her, kiss her, hold her as he'd held her so many times before. Instead, he stood up and waved, and she walked slowly over. There was a look of wariness on her face.

'Hi,' he said. 'Thanks for coming. Coffee? Tea?'

'Nothing,' she said.

She sat down.

'So,' she said. 'Unconventional science.'

'Or maybe hallucination,' said Jake. 'At least, that's what the doctor at the department said. Caused by a leak of toxic gas.'

Lauren didn't reply, just sat waiting for Jake to go on.

'This isn't easy for me,' said Jake.

'Nor for me,' said Lauren. She hesitated, and looked as if she was about to say something personal. Her eyes still held that wounded look he'd seen in them at the wedding. But instead she sighed and said, 'Let's stick to the science, Jake.'

Jake nodded, and he told her what had happened, starting with the protestors and the 'fairy ring', and then the actual events at the building site: the construction worker turning into something inhuman. And about his feelings that his department was trying to conceal something. All the while Lauren listened, and Jake was relieved to notice that her expression had softened as he talked, her eyes showing curiosity.

'There was nothing on the news about this,' she said, when he'd finished. 'Or on the web.'

'The department put a Schedule D notice on the story,' said Jake. 'A news blackout.'

'And where do I come in?' asked Lauren.

'Because I thought it was your kind of thing,' said Jake. 'Odd stuff. I mean, say it wasn't a hallucination but it was real. It *felt* real. It still feels real.'

'And how would you know if it was?'

Jake hesitated, then asked, 'Have you ever heard of Sigma?'

Lauren nodded.

'It's a letter of the Greek alphabet.'

'Not the Greek alphabet one. It could be a code or something. Maybe a secret organisation.'

Lauren shook her head.

'How about Malichea . . . ?'

'The Order of Malichea?'

Jake could tell she was intrigued by his mentioning the word. He shrugged.

'I don't know,' said Jake. 'Possibly. It was a word written in a report about this incident in the files at the department.'

'The reference might make sense, if it is,' mused Lauren. 'I wanted to write a thesis on the Order of

Malichea, but my professor said the subject wasn't academic enough. In fact, he said it was more suitable for science fiction.'

'Why?'

Lauren shrugged.

'Narrow-minded, I guess, like much of the scientific establishment.'

'Well . . . who are they? This . . . Order of Malichea?'

'Were,' corrected Lauren. 'They were a religious order, or semi-religious, devoted to the study of science. In particular, what were called "heretical sciences". Things that didn't fit with what the Church said. They died out soon after 1536. Henry VIII and the dissolution of the monasteries, remember?'

'Not particularly,' said Jake. 'Religion was never my strong point. So they . . . what? Looked into this kind of thing?'

Lauren nodded.

'More than looked into it. They collected this kind of thing. Science texts from all over the world, especially the Arab world, which was way ahead of the West scientifically in the eighth and ninth centuries. Which did not go down well with the Church of the time, or later. Remember the Inquisition?'

Jake grinned.

'Yes,' he said. 'Monty Python. Everyone remembers the Spanish Inquisition.'

Lauren gave him a stern look.

'I'm being serious,' she said. 'The Inquisition wasn't confined to Spain. So, according to legend, the Order of Malichea hid all the science texts somewhere safe so that they wouldn't be destroyed by the Church. And not just the Church. Certain kings also thought some of these scientific ideas were dangerous and ought to be suppressed. Many of these sciences were thought of as subversive.'

'Why?'

'Because they questioned the orthodox theory of how the world worked. Remember, even in the twentieth century such books were banned. The Nazis ordered them burned. The Catholic Church also ordered them destroyed. Anything that contradicted the official line on how the universe was made and worked. And these books weren't just doing things like claiming that the sun orbited the earth and not the other way round, as Galileo said, and which was thought of as a terrible heresy, for which he was killed. When you think the library of the Order of Malichea was said to have books on subjects like invisibility; turning ordinary metal into gold; the quest for eternal life; raising the dead . . .'

'Sorcery and witchcraft,' said Jake.

'Exactly.' Lauren nodded. 'And even more so when you add books on time travel, mind-reading, levitation, telekinesis . . .'

'Telekinesis?' queried Jake.

'Moving things just by using the power of your mind,' clarified Lauren. 'Then there were said to be texts on genetic engineering, seeing into the future . . .'

'Dangerous stuff.'

'Very. It's said that if this library actually existed and the sciences had been put into practice, we'd have been on the moon five hundred years before we actually were. Plus treatments would have been found by now for most diseases.' She thought for a bit, then added, 'I've actually still got my notes on the Order of Malichea. I've thought about writing a book about them, if I can find a sympathetic publisher, that is. The problem is, I want it to be a proper book, not some weirdo thing for fantasy geeks, and that's not going to be easy.'

'You think there might be some kind of connection?' asked Jake hopefully. 'Between this order and what I saw?'

'What you *may* have seen,' corrected Lauren. 'Although the thing that makes me think there might be a connection is the business of the fairy ring.'

Jake frowned at her, checking to see if she was winding him up in some way, but she didn't appear to be making a joke.

'The fairy ring?' he queried.

'It's said the Order of Malichea hid their whole library,' she said. 'They didn't want it to fall into the hands of the establishment, where it could be destroyed. And, to make sure that no one dug it up accidentally, the books were spread around the whole country and buried in places that were rumoured to be holy, or haunted, or sacred, or cursed.'

'Places where no one was likely to dig,' said Jake. 'Like a so-called fairy ring.'

'Exactly.' Lauren nodded. She looked at her watch and stood up. 'I've got to go.'

'I thought you said you were free the rest of the day,' blurted out Jake helplessly, then shut up.

Lauren looked awkward. 'I'm meeting someone,' she said. There was a pause, then she added, 'Actually, I'm seeing someone these days.'

'Robert the rugby player?' asked Jake, doing his best to appear casual.

Lauren glared at him, her eyes blazing angrily.

'You idiot!' she snapped. 'Robert is my cousin! He and I have played together since we were about two years old! He is also very happily engaged to a good friend of mine and getting married this year!'

Jake dropped his eyes, shamefaced.

'I'm sorry,' he said.

'So you should be!'

There was a pause, then Lauren added, 'If you must know, the man I'm seeing is another student at the university. He's a third year. Very intelligent. Very mature.'

Mentally, Jake kicked himself. Robert was her cousin! And because of what he thought was going on, he'd messed up big time. And now, he'd lost her to some mature Brainiac!

'I'm . . . glad for you,' he said, forcing the words out and doing his best to smile. To break the awkward pause that followed, he asked, 'So, this stuff you've got on the Order of Malichea . . .'

Lauren nodded.

'It's on my laptop. I'll email it to you. Is your email address still the same?'

Jake nodded, but said hopefully, 'Or we could always meet up . . .'

'No, I don't think that would be a good idea. I'll email it you,' said Lauren. 'I'll do it later today.'

'OK,' said Jake. He got up. They stood looking at one another, awkwardly, and then Jake leant forward and planted a chaste kiss on Lauren's cheek.

'I'm sorry,' he said quietly.

'So am I,' she said.

Then she turned and walked away. Jake sat down again and watched her go. With you, you take my heart, he thought numbly.

# Chapter 6

Jake spent the rest of the afternoon in a bit of a daze. He went to a gallery, but he couldn't remember what he saw. He went to the South Bank, where there was a free concert happening, but if anyone had asked him afterwards who or even what had been playing, he wouldn't have been able to say. All he could think of was the fact that Robert had been Lauren's cousin, her childhood playpal, and he'd screwed it up. Lauren flicking her fingers through Robert's hair and laughing, claiming she was looking for nits. Of course! That's what kids did! It had been real family affection between them. That's why Robert had called on him and threatened him. Not because he wanted Lauren for himself, but to protect Lauren. Jake had been such an idiot! No, not just an idiot! A Grade A Oscar-Winning Idiot.

By early evening, Jake was feeling so depressed he could almost describe it as suicidal. But what would be the point of that? It wouldn't get Lauren back. He wondered if it was the effects of the gas making him feel like this. But then he remembered there hadn't been any gas, despite what Gareth and the doctor had told him. He *knew* there hadn't been any gas. And this business of the Order of Malichea seemed to make the whole thing even clearer. There was a cover-up going on. And someone had tried to push him under a train!

Oh God, don't start on that direction! he groaned to himself. Not another conspiracy! 'Aliens ate my brother!' 'All World Leaders are Lizards!'

But there *was* something going on. Malichea. Sigma. The construction worker. And someone *had* tried to push him under the train. Jake was sure it was not just coincidence that it had happened after Gareth had spotted him in the archive library.

Jake thought about what Lauren had told him about this Order of Malichea hiding their library in places that were rumoured to be holy, or haunted, or sacred, or cursed. Like a fairy ring. Was it really possible . . . ?

His mobile rang. He checked the number on the screen. It was Lauren! Hastily, he made the connection.

'Hi,' he said, smiling to himself. She was calling him!

'It's Lauren!' said Lauren, and she sounded seriously angry, and the smile vanished from Jake's face as he

47

wondered what he could have said or done to upset her. But then she said, 'I've been burgled!'

'What?' said Jake, his mind in a whirl. His first thought was one of relief that she wasn't angry at him over what had happened, but her next words put an end to that feeling of relief.

'Who have you been talking to about me?' she demanded.

'What?' stumbled Jake. 'No one? Why?'

'Because they took my laptop! And my notepads with my notes!'

'What notes?'

'All of them. Including my notes on the Order of Malichea! Why would anyone do that?'

'I don't know,' stammered Jake.

'Because they knew what you were asking me!' said Lauren accusingly. 'You must have told someone!'

'I swear, I haven't told anyone!' insisted Jake. 'I only picked up the word Malichea this morning for the first time, at my department. The only person I mentioned it to was the librarian in the archives library . . .'

And immediately afterwards, Gareth turned up in the library, thought Jake. Gareth, who never ventures below the third floor. Gareth, who if he wants anything from the archives sends a minion to get it.

'Jake . . . !' came Lauren's voice. 'Are you still there?'

'Yes,' said Jake. 'Lauren, I don't think we should say anything more over the phone right now. There's something going on.'

'And you think my burglary's proof of it?'

'Yes. I think it could well be.'

There was a pause, and Jake could hear Lauren talking, but muffled, and someone more distant replying. She wasn't alone.

'Lauren . . .' he began.

'Wait a minute,' she said.

There was more talking at the other end of the phone, too muffled for him to hear, then she said, 'The South Bank. One of the benches near the Festival Hall by the bridge.'

'Got it,' he said. 'When?'

'An hour. We'll see you there.'

'We?' he queried.

'After this, I'm not coming to see you on my own. If you're right, I'm going to need protection.'

With that she hung up. Jake wondered who she would be bringing with her. She'd said 'protection'. That suggested Robert, that huge hulking rugby player cousin of hers. The big question was: who had burgled Lauren's flat? Circumstances pointed to Gareth being involved in some way. But why? And why take the stuff on the Order of Malichea?

# Chapter 7

Jake sat on the bench on the South Bank in front of the Festival Hall and looked at the familiar landmarks along the Thames. The tower of the OXO building. The Savoy. The three bridges nearby spanning the Thames: the ancient rusted metal of the Hungerford railway bridge; the gleaming new shininess of the footbridge, and, further away to his right, the white stone walls of Waterloo Bridge. He remembered times when he and Lauren had sat here at this very spot, watching the lights sparkling on the waters of the Thames. Those had been the early days of their relationship, when they had been so happy together.

He shook his head to shake the image out of his mind. Stop thinking of her like that. A hand on his shoulder made him jump, and he half rose, half turned, and there she was, as beautiful as ever. But the man with her wasn't Robert the rugby player. He was much smaller. Thinner, with a wisp of a moustache, and in his early twenties.

'Jake, this is Carl Parsons.'

Of course. The new boyfriend. The Mature Brainiac.

Jake stood up and shook Parsons's hand, though something inside him wanted to crush it. He was surprised at how firm the handshake was, coming from such a weedy-looking individual.

'I've told Carl the story you told me,' said Lauren as they both joined Jake sitting down on the bench. 'About the building worker turning into something.'

'Yes.' Parsons nodded. 'Intriguing.'

'Carl's in the same department as me, studying Theoretical Sciences,' explained Lauren.

Jake couldn't resist thinking sarcastically: *He's* your protection? Aloud, he said, 'Did you report the burglary to the police?'

'Of course,' said Lauren. 'Waste of time though. They're convinced it was just some junkies breaking in looking for money for drugs.'

'And taking your information on the Order of Malichea instead?' commented Jake.

'They homed in on Lauren's laptop,' said Parsons. 'They said laptops were a prime target. Easily portable.'

'And the notes you said they took?' asked Jake.

Lauren shook her head.

'I don't think they even bothered to write that down,' she said. 'They concentrated on the laptop and a CD player the burglars also took. For them that was proof it was just junkies.'

'A CD player?' queried Jake.

'Obvious cover,' said Parsons. 'If they'd really been junkies they'd have taken the TV as well.'

'Maybe it was too big?' suggested Jake.

'So, you believe what the police say?' asked Lauren.

Jake shook his head.

'No,' he said. 'Your notes being taken is the crucial pointer. They want to eliminate everything about the Order of Malichea completely, make sure you have nothing.'

'But that's stupid!' exploded Lauren angrily. 'Stuff about the Order is all over the internet! All anyone's got to do is a Google search and it's there!'

Jake frowned. He wished he'd thought of that before. But there was still one puzzle, if what Lauren said was true: why was the information on his department's search engine restricted to Level 4 security and above? The answer had to be: because the information in the department's archives was more detailed than anything anyone would find on the internet.

'I think they're trying to scare you off,' said Parsons.

They both looked at him.

'It's logical when you think about it,' Parsons continued. 'The information you had about the Order is on the internet . . .'

'Not all of it,' interrupted Lauren. 'Basic stuff, the history of the Order, that sort of thing, but some of my research came from other sources. Old books, libraries . . .'

'And you could get hold of it again,' persisted Parsons. 'And whoever these people were know that. So I think this is a message, and a not very subtle one, warning you to keep out of this.'

'Why?' asked Lauren. 'Why send *me* that message and not Jake? He's the one poking his nose in.'

'They already sent me a message of sorts,' said Jake. 'Someone tried to kill me.'

'What?' Lauren looked at Jake, disbelief on her face. 'Oh, come on . . . !'

'No, I'm serious,' said Jake hastily. 'Someone tried to push me under a train this morning at Victoria.'

'The platform must have just been crowded,' said Lauren. 'People always push.'

'That's what I thought,' agreed Jake. 'But someone definitely pushed me, not just a little push, but a hard push. And they did it twice.' He looked thoughtful. 'I must admit, I still wasn't completely convinced it wasn't just some accident, or some lunatic, until you told me about your burglary.'

53

Lauren and Parsons exchanged looks. Then Parsons said, 'I know it sounds far-fetched, but there have been instances of the government shutting people up by arranging accidents.'

Jake looked at Parsons in surprise. This was support from a very unexpected quarter.

'But why would they burgle my flat?' asked Lauren.

'Because you know about the Order of Malichea,' said Parsons. 'Jake doesn't. It's a warning. They don't want you helping him to find out more.'

'Why should they think I would help him?'

'You already were,' pointed out Parsons. 'You said to Jake you'd email him the information you had about the Order, remember? You told me so.'

'Yes, but I only told you and Jake,' said Lauren. 'So how would they know that?'

'Bugs,' said Jake. 'Eavesdropping equipment. Telephone taps.'

Parsons nodded. 'That's quite possible,' he said.

'No, it's not,' Lauren said. 'I said that to Jake in the precinct in front of the British Library, out in the open air, and unless the table we were sitting at was bugged . . .'

'Directional microphones,' said Parsons. 'State-of-the-art surveillance equipment. Parabolic mics. You can pick up a conversation in the open air from fifty metres. Even further with the latest technology.'

Lauren looked shocked. She shook her head. 'But how would anyone know that we were worth bugging?'

'Because of what happened to me this morning, getting kicked out of the department,' said Jake. 'It was me they were bugging, waiting to see who I contacted. And I contacted you.' He gave an apologetic sigh. 'I'm sorry. I didn't mean to drag you into this. Well . . . I did, but I didn't think it would lead to this. I'm really sorry.'

'I'm not,' said Lauren.

Jake looked at her in surprise.

'But . . .' he began. Lauren didn't let him finish.

'I've always wanted to write a book about the Order of Malichea. This is all about what you could call "lost sciences". Science books that the Order hid hundreds of years ago because the sciences in them were deemed "dangerous" by the powers that be. As far as I knew, all the evidence about the Order of Malichea and their lost sciences was circumstantial, stories with some evidence to back them up, but nothing tangible. Nothing solid. *This* is solid.'

Jake frowned, puzzled.

'I don't get you,' he said.

'The event that happened in Bedfordshire, the building worker turning into something weird,' said Lauren 'You saw that.'

'Yes,' said Jake. 'I swear I did.'

'The attempts by this boss of yours . . .'

'Gareth Findlay-Weston.' Jake nodded.

'. . . by him to persuade you it was all a hallucination. And now this burglary, my laptop and my notes on the Order of Malichea being taken as a warning. It means there *is* hard evidence, and someone's got it, and they don't want it being known about as real instead of just some . . . weird stuff.'

'You're jumping to a bit of a conclusion,' said Parsons doubtfully.

'I am – a logical conclusion,' said Lauren.

'A *circumstantial* conclusion,' challenged Parsons.

Good, thought Jake. Please argue between you.

'I know what's happened so far points to that, but there could be another explanation which we're missing, because we don't have all the information,' insisted Parsons. 'And there's another thing . . .' and he began to look around, concerned. 'We've just agreed that it's likely your conversation outside the British Library was bugged. So what's the betting the same people are listening to us at this very moment?'

Lauren and Jake exchanged concerned looks. Parsons was right. Then Lauren's expression changed to one of angry determination. It was an expression Jake recognised all too well. It was the expression she'd had on her face when she'd told him he could go to hell after she'd found him with the bridesmaid.

'Then we're going to change that,' she said. She stood up. 'Come on.'

'Where are we going?' asked Parsons.

'Where we can talk without being overheard.'

# Chapter 8

As Jake and Parsons followed Lauren across the pedestrian bridge over the Thames towards Embankment Station they kept a resolute silence, to Jake's great frustration. Where are we going? he thought. Surely it wouldn't do any harm for her to at least tell me where we're heading. We're walking on a bridge over the Thames; no one can pick up what we say here. Unless we had a parabolic microphone trained on us from a boat on the Thames. What were the chances of that?

Every chance, realised Jake gloomily. These people tried to kill me, they've taken Lauren's laptop. They can get everywhere and do anything.

He kept silent, along with the other two, and just followed them. From the Embankment they caught a train to Baron's Court. Outside the station Lauren hailed a taxi.

'It's only a short distance from here,' she whispered. 'But this way, if anyone has been following us, it should throw them off the scent.'

Under Lauren's directions, the taxi turned off the main road, and then zigzagged through back streets, until she gave the order for it to pull up.

They were outside a small terraced house. Lauren rang the doorbell. After a few moments the door opened and the massive figure of Robert, Lauren's rugby-playing cousin, looked out at them. He grinned massively when he saw Lauren, but then his look fell on Jake and he scowled.

'What's he doing here?' he growled.

'Later, Robert,' said Lauren. 'Can we come in? It's urgent.'

Robert stepped aside and the three slipped into the house.

Jake expected the inside of the house to be the sort he expected from a hulking great rugby player like Robert: namely, a rubbish tip, with rugby boots and shorts and empty beer cans dumped all over the place. To his surprise, the interior was neat and tidy. And not just neat, it was very tastefully decorated, and quite modern in a minimalist style.

'Nice place,' murmured Jake, looking around at the room they had walked into in.

'Robert's an architect,' said Lauren.

Jake looked in surprise at Robert as he joined them. This hulking great man-mountain of a rugby player, someone who looked like he could tear an opponent apart with his bare hands, was an architect?

'What's up?' demanded Lauren. 'You're looking strange.'

'Nothing,' said Jake quickly. 'I'm just a bit knocked over by all that's going on.' He shook his head. 'I can't believe this is happening.'

'Oh, it is,' said Parsons quietly. 'What we have to find out is where you fit in.'

'Tea or coffee anyone?' asked Robert.

'Decaf coffee for me,' said Lauren.

'Tea for me, please, Robert,' said Parsons.

Parsons has been here before, thought Jake. He's a friend of Robert's now. Part of the family, he thought bitterly.

'You?' Robert demanded of Jake, his voice still menacing enough to make Jake worry.

'Me, what?' asked Jake, uncertainly.

'Tea or coffee?'

'Er . . . tea, please. If that's OK.'

Robert glowered at him, then disappeared into the kitchen.

'Right,' said Lauren, sitting down on the settee. 'Tell Carl what you told me. About what you saw.'

'You said you'd already told him?' said Jake, puzzled.

'Yes, but I want him to hear it from you in case I missed something out.'

So Jake repeated the story to Carl Parsons: the fairy ring, the digger, the worker suddenly being covered with vegetation, the panic, the SAS team arriving, the ambulances, him being ordered home on sick leave by his boss. And the attempt on his life at the underground station.

While Jake was telling his story, Robert appeared with a tray with their drinks on and set them down on the small coffee table, before sitting down with them and joining in listening to Jake.

When Jake had finished, Lauren turned to Parsons. 'Well?' she asked.

'Sounds like fungal spores,' murmured Parsons.

'In particular, El Izmir and the greening of the desert,' added Lauren.

'And not just the text but the actual spores,' added Parsons thoughtfully. He shook his head, an expression of awe on his face. 'It's not possible, is it? That the fungal spores were actually placed by El Izmir inside the pages of the book?'

Jake looked from Lauren to Parsons, and then back at Lauren again.

'Would either of you mind telling me what you're talking about?' he demanded, annoyed. 'I'm out of the loop here.'

'It's a treatise said to have been written in about 690 AD by El Izmir Al Tabul, an Arabian philosopher and agrarianist,' answered Lauren.

'Agrarianist?' asked Jake, with a puzzled frown.

'A gardener,' explained Parsons.

'Then why not say so,' Jake complained, 'instead of using words like some sort of code to cut me out and make me feel like a spare part.'

'I'm not trying to make you feel cut out,' defended Lauren. 'The fact is, he was more than just a gardener, and – for me – science is about being precise. Anyway, when I was researching the Order of Malichea I came across a list of books that were said to have been in the secret library.'

'I think I need to know more about this secret library,' said Jake.

'Bear with me' said Lauren. 'One of the books was a scientific text written in the late seventh century by this El Izmir, in which he claimed to have developed a strain of fungus that only needed the moisture in air in which to grow rapidly. As soon as the dehydrated spores came into contact with moisture . . . voom!'

'And the point of this was?'

'Food,' put in Parsons. 'The desert is not a place where food can be cultivated easily, and in areas far from groundwater, but where there could be moisture in the air . . .'

'OK, I get the idea.' Jake nodded. 'So this particular type of fungus . . .'

'Was an early example of genetic modification of a plant strain,' said Lauren. 'Food that could be grown in abundance from the water in air.'

'If it's true, that would be fantastic,' said Jake. 'Growing food rich in protein in desert areas.'

'An end to famine,' said Robert.

'Exactly!' said Lauren.

'But it didn't happen,' pointed out Jake.

'It did,' said Lauren. 'You saw it happen. The fungus grew when exposed to air.'

Jake shook his head.

'It grew on this man who was working at the site,' he said.

'Because human beings are seventy per cent moisture,' said Parsons.

'The spores have to be released in a properly controlled way,' added Lauren.

Jake thought about it, and what he'd seen. The man opening the book, breathing in whatever was stuck to the pages.

'You're right,' he said. Then he frowned. 'But, if it works, why hasn't anyone heard about it before? I mean, something like this, that could solve hunger . . .'

'Because El Izmir's book about the fungus was

destroyed, along with the rest of the secret library,' said Lauren. 'Or, it was *believed* to have been destroyed.'

'We'd better tell him about the secret library and the Order of Malichea,' said Parsons. 'Otherwise none of this is going to make sense.'

Lauren turned to Robert.

'Robert, have you still got that battered old van of yours?' she asked.

Robert looked affronted.

'Lizzie is not a battered old van,' he replied defensively. 'All right, she may have a few dents here and there, but . . .'

'But is she still noisy?'

Robert looked uncomfortable.

'Well, compared to some of these *modern* vehicles . . .' he began, his tone a definite sneer.

'Good,' said Lauren. 'We'll need your laptop.'

'OK,' said Robert. 'I'll go and get it.'

# Chapter 9

Lauren waited until they were all in Robert's van and he'd turned over the ignition and started it up before she told them her plan. Robert was at the wheel, Jake was in the back of the van with Lauren and Parsons. The van was really noisy. Lauren had to shout to make herself heard above the sound of the engine.

'Once, when my laptop was out of commission, I borrowed Robert's and copied my files on to it,' she said.

She opened Robert's laptop, turned it on, and her fingers began hitting keys.

'So he has the history of the Order of Malichea on it?' asked Parsons.

'Providing he hasn't deleted it,' said Lauren.

'I haven't,' Robert called from the front of the van. 'Everything you put on there is still there, just in case you needed it.'

As the van set off and began chugging along the road, Jake realised why Lauren had chosen it for this session. There would be very few microphones, if any, that would be able to pick up their conversation above the noisy engine.

Lauren found the file she was looking for and passed the laptop to Jake.

'Read this,' she said.

' "The Order of Malichea and the Lost Sciences", by Lauren Graham,' read Jake.

'In the seventh and eighth centuries, the monastery at Lindisfarne on Holy Island, off the east coast of Britain, was the centre for all learning. Scholars from across the whole of the known world, from Europe, Asia and north Africa, came to Lindisfarne to exchange researches on a huge range of topics, especially the sciences. They brought their notebooks, and the monks at the monastery made copies for the monastery library. By AD 780, the library at Lindisfarne held most scientific knowledge available at that time. An order dedicated to the development of science sprang up within the larger order at Lindisfarne. This was the Order of Malichea.

'In 793, the monks at Lindisfarne heard a rumour that the Vikings were preparing to invade Britain. The monks were afraid that the Vikings would come to Holy Island, and if they did they'd destroy the library with all these precious scientific texts. It's believed that some members of the Order of Malichea decided to take all the scientific texts away to a sympathetic abbey at Caen in Normandy, in northern France, where the library found safe haven. In 793, the Vikings did invade Holy Island, as had been predicted, and they destroyed the priory at Lindisfarne before they went on to attack the rest of Britain. But the science books were now safe in France.

'From 793, the library of scientific texts, now held by the Order of Malichea at the abbey at Caen, were added to, with scientists from all faiths, all nations.

'In 1130, the Norman Roger became Roger II, King of Sicily, succeeding his father and brother. Roger unified three separate faiths under his rule: Christian, Byzantine and Islam; and encouraged scholars from all three cultures to contribute their scholarship and knowledge to his kingdom. As a result, as had happened at Lindisfarne hundreds of years earlier, the library of the court of Roger II included works of scholarship – particularly scientific – from all cultures, particularly Islamic. The library expanded under Roger's successors: William I, II and III, and Tancred. However, the Pope considered the kingdom of Sicily, where Islam was on equal terms to Christianity, to be a "heathen" kingdom and ordered crusades to destroy it.

'Although many of the texts of the library of Roger II survived, including works by Ptolomy and Islamic scholars, those that were considered particularly heretical had already been smuggled out of Sicily and taken to the abbey at Caen, where they were added to the scientific library of the Order of Malichea.

'By the middle of the fifteenth century, the library of the Order of Malichea in the abbey at Caen was the hub of all knowledge of the global scientific community. However, the abbot of the Order was acutely aware that to the Establishment of the time, both Church and State, these works could be considered dangerous.

'In 1483, the Inquisition was set up in Spain under Tomás de Torquemada, to seek out and destroy heresy. That included all heretical writing and thought. The Inquisition spread beyond Spain to Italy, and there were fears that it would spread through the rest of Continental Europe.

'The monks of the Order of Malichea at the abbey in Caen were very worried: many of the scientific works in their library were by Arabic or Islamic scholars, and many dated from pre-Christian Roman or Greek times. For that reason alone, most of them would be considered heretical, and would be destroyed, as would any texts that went against the orthodox Church view of the world. In order to save the texts from destruction, they moved the library again. A large party of monks was sent to Britain, under the guise of making a pilgrimage to Glastonbury, because the abbot at Glastonbury was sympathetic to the Order of Malichea. Each monk took with him a number of books. And at Glastonbury Abbey they hid the library in secret rooms behind the official library.

'Unfortunately, even at Glastonbury the books weren't safe, because over the years the threat of the Inquisition spread, and the Church in Britain also began to seek out and destroy heretical thinking in its ranks. So, in 1497 the leader of the Order of Malichea took drastic action to save the texts. The monks of the Order were told to take these so-called "heretical" science books and hide them, secreting each in a separate place. To ensure the books would not be discovered, each one was to be hidden in a place that was unlikely to be disturbed because it was either sacred, or said to be cursed, or claimed to be haunted. A coded list of the different books and their hiding places was kept, known as The Index.

'The abbot's intention was for the books to stay hidden until the threat of the Inquisition had passed, and then the books could be recovered and returned to the abbey library in safety. However, the Inquisition didn't pass. As far as the authorities were concerned, anything considered heretical had to be destroyed. So the books stayed hidden.

'In 1498, plague returned to Britain and wiped out a huge percentage of the population, including many of the monks who had hidden the scientific texts. With them went the knowledge of where they'd hidden them. The only evidence that these "lost sciences" actually existed and had been hidden were in the *Journal of the Order of Malichea*, which was a history of the Order handed down through the ages since AD 780, and The Index, the supposed list of where the scientific books were hidden.

'In 1536, Henry VIII ordered the Dissolution of the Monasteries. Although many monasteries and abbeys capitulated to the king's forces, the Abbot of Glastonbury, Richard Whiting, refused to allow the king's troops to enter the abbey when they arrived to take possession in 1539. As a result of Whiting's defiance he was hanged, drawn and quartered as a traitor at Glastonbury Tor on 15 November 1539. Henry VIII's forces then sacked the abbey, and the books in the priory's library, including the *Journal of the Order of Malichea*, came into the hands of the king, and so into the possession of the State. But it's not known what happened to The Index. It may have been destroyed during the attack by the king's men on Glastonbury. *The Journal of the Order of Malichea* has also since "disappeared", though whether it is still in the archives of the State is a matter of conjecture.'

\*      \*      \*

Jake passed the laptop back to Lauren, who turned it off and closed it down.

'If what was dug up *is* the hidden text by El Izmir, then this is the first proof that the secret library of forbidden books existed and was hidden,' said Lauren.

'As far as we know,' added Parsons thoughtfully. 'Others may have been found before that, and put in storage somewhere.'

'But why would anyone want to keep this information hidden?' asked Jake. 'Like you say, this fungus stuff could end world hunger.'

'It could also be used as a biological weapon,' said Parsons. 'You saw that yourself. Imagine those same fungal spores, but a million of them, used as a weapon.'

'Yes, but everything is a potential weapon!' exploded Jake. 'A pencil in the wrong hands can be used to stab someone! You can't do nothing just because something could be dangerous.'

'Jake's right,' said Lauren, giving Jake a smile. Both the smile and the words sent a thrill through him. 'This is our opportunity to expose the truth. Not just about this book, but the proof that the secret library existed, and is hidden out there. And the secrets the books hold could bring untold wonders to the world. End famine. Cure diseases.'

'And also be used as weapons in the wrong hands,' repeated Parsons.

'Then we have to make sure the information gets into the right hands,' insisted Lauren.

'How?' asked Parsons. 'The book by El Izmir will be under lock and key by now, you can be sure of that.'

'So, we find another one,' said Lauren.

'How?' asked Jake, puzzled.

'We explore the sites I listed, the possible hiding places where the books were hidden, until we find one of the books. We only need to find one to prove that the secret library existed and was hidden. And then we can launch a search for the rest.'

Jake looked from her to Parsons, and then back to Lauren again.

'It's a bit of a long shot,' he said. 'According to everything you've found out, they've been hidden for hundreds of years, but this is the first time one's actually been found. Trying to find another one could take . . . well . . . years.'

'And there is the problem that most of them will be buried on land that is protected,' said Parsons thoughtfully.

Lauren looked affronted.

'You're agreeing with Jake?' she demanded.

'In this case, yes.' Parsons nodded.

Great, thought Jake delightedly. They're splitting up, and over me! OK, not in the way I'd hoped, but it's a start.

'I think we need to concentrate on getting the El Izmir book back,' said Parsons.

'And how do you propose we do that?' asked Lauren.

'We use Jake,' said Parsons. 'After all, it's his department that's got it.'

As Parsons's words sunk in, Jake felt a sense of panic creeping over him. No! he thought. The last time I tried nosing around within my department about this, someone tried to kill me!

'No, I think Lauren's right,' he said. 'I take back what I said. I think we ought to start again, just as Lauren said. There will be more books out there, hidden. I'm sure we can find one.'

Parsons didn't seem convinced.

'In my opinion, you were right first time, Jake,' he said. 'Trying to find another one could take . . . well . . . years. This offers our best opportunity.'

'Yes,' agreed Lauren. 'That makes sense.'

Beaten with my own words! thought Jake gloomily. 'OK.' He nodded.

From the front of the van, Robert called out, 'How much longer do you want me to keep driving around. Lizzie soaks up fuel like a sponge. I'm going to have

73

to find a petrol station if we're going to go on much longer.'

'We're finished, thanks, Robert!' called Lauren. To Jake she said, 'Right, it's up to you, Jake. You have to find out where they've taken the book!'

# Chapter 10

As Jake walked through the imposing entrance of the Department of Science at 9 a.m. on Thursday morning – his twenty-four-hour sojourn over – his mind was in turmoil. *Find out where they've taken the book!* Lauren's instructions screamed at him. Impossible!

He'd spent the whole of the last day thinking about it. *Worrying* about it.

Gareth knew he'd been digging into the Order of Malichea, he was sure of it. He had discovered him in the archives, and Jake was certain he would have asked the clerks there what Jake had been looking for. Gareth had sent him home. And it had been on his way home that someone had tried to push him under a tube train. The connection was obvious, and it sent shivers down his spine. Gareth was behind the attempt to kill him.

And now he was going back into the lion's den. Back into this building where Gareth ruled the roost and could order him to go here or there, to places that could be dangerous. Over the past two days Jake's mind had played out all sorts of scenarios. Gareth calling Jake and sending him on an assignment to a steelworks somewhere, where he could suffer an accident with molten metal and be killed. Although his own awareness of UK industry told him that nearly all the steelworks in Britain had closed down and most steel production now went on in India. He couldn't see Gareth sending him out to Mumbai to have him killed – too expensive, especially with the taxpayer footing the bill.

A road accident, thought Jake. That's how most political assassinations seemed to be carried out. Car crashes. People run over on pedestrian crossings. But only low-level people, of course. Jake couldn't believe that anyone important would actually be *walking* anywhere, let alone across a pedestrian crossing. Important people were driven everywhere. Walking in London was for low-level civil servants. People like Jake. So, for the past twenty-four hours, Jake had spent most of his time in his flat. When he did go out, like this morning to go to work, he made sure that he only crossed a road if there was a crowd of people crossing at the same time.

I'm getting paranoid, he thought. Especially since Lauren gave me all that stuff to read. The hidden books.

Henry VIII killing the Abbot of Glastonbury. We've got a long tradition of political assassinations in this country, thought Jake.

'Jake!'

The voice stopped him short as he crossed the marble entrance hall to the stairs. It was Gareth Findlay-Weston. Why was he here? Had he been deliberately waiting for Jake?

Jake fought to keep down the feeling of panic welling up in him and turned to face Gareth as he came to him.

'You're back.' Gareth smiled.

No thanks to you, thought Jake acidly.

Gareth's face suddenly went into an expression of deep concern.

'How are you, Jake?' he asked.

'I'm fine, thank you, Gareth.'

'No recurrence of the . . . the problem?'

Jake forced what he hoped sounded like a light laugh.

'No,' he said. Then he put on his best sincere expression. 'I'm so sorry about what happened. Thinking I was seeing things at that site, I mean.' He gave what he hoped was a rueful chuckle. 'A man turning into a vegetable! God! I must have seemed like a complete loon.'

Gareth visibly relaxed.

'I must admit, you had us all worried.'

'Luckily, the pills the doctor gave me sorted me out. They must have flushed the toxic whatever it was – the gases – through my system.'

'So, no after-effects?'

Jake shook his head.

'No. The brain's back in working order.' He smiled. 'No little green men or flying elephants.'

'Excellent!' Gareth beamed. He clapped Jake heartily on the shoulder. 'The department will be very relieved to have you back! That incident the other day really set the cat among the pigeons! You know . . .'

'The hallucinogenic stuff,' finished Jake with a rueful sigh. He forced a smile. 'Luckily, as I experienced it myself, I might be able to answer some of the questions. Scotch any rumours and gossip.'

'Good man! That's what I like to hear!' Then Gareth put on his concerned face again. 'But if you do start to feel anything odd . . .'

'Don't worry, I'll get down to the medicos straight away,' Jake reassured him. 'But, honestly, I feel fine.'

With that, he gave Gareth a last smile, and then headed for the stairs. The man was a lying hypocrite, he thought. But how do I find out what he knows? How do I find out where the book was taken?

Paul Evans was talking on the phone as Jake walked into the office. He hung up as he saw Jake and grinned at him.

'Aha, here's the man who sees things that aren't there!' he chuckled.

'Don't remind me,' said Jake with a wry grin. 'I must have sounded like I was out of my head.' Then, as casually as he could, he asked, 'Did they actually find out what it was? The toxic gas stuff that made us all see things?'

Paul shook his head.

'Not yet,' he said. 'But I'm sure they will once they've examined the canister.'

'What canister?' asked Jake, suddenly alert. There had been no canister. Just a book.

'The one that was dug up,' said Paul. 'Apparently, the digger must have fractured it. They reckon it contained some kind of nerve gas, possibly left over from the Second World War. Anyway, they've taken it to Aylesbury for examination.'

A surge of excitement went through Jake. Maybe this was just the latest in a series of red herrings, but there was also the possibility that whatever had been found in that hole *had* been taken somewhere.

'What's at Aylesbury?' he asked, doing his best to make his voice sound casual.

Paul shrugged.

'Some kind of chemical research lab,' he said. 'I'd have thought they'd have taken it to Porton Down, but I guess Aylesbury was nearer.'

'Well, I for one will be keen to find out what was in it!' said Jake. 'I breathed in a great whiff of it, which was what sent me off my head and got me seeing things.'

'A man turning into a vegetable!' chuckled Paul.

'You can laugh! You wouldn't have found it so funny if it had been you seeing walking vegetables!' protested Jake, but doing his best to keep his tone jokey. He mustn't appear too keen, too eager; that would only raise suspicion. The last thing he wanted was Paul mentioning anything that might get back to Gareth and set some danger in motion. He still felt a shiver go through him when he thought of that hand pushing him towards the oncoming tube train.

'I doubt if we'll ever know,' said Paul. 'You know what these science types are like – they like to keep everything close to their chests.'

'Surely they'll publish a report,' said Jake.

'Yes, but it will be TLEO: for Top Level Eyes Only.'

'Drat!' said Jake. 'Now I'll never know what infected me.' He put on a petulant tone. 'So how do I know if I ought to take precautions?'

'About what? It happening again?'

'No, about it conflicting with some future medication. You know, if I'm going abroad and I have to have injections, and they ask me if I've suffered from some kind of illness in the past, just to make sure there isn't a cross-reaction.'

80

'Oh, I'm sure they'd tell you if that was a possibility,' said Paul.

'I bet they don't,' said Jake. 'Like you say, these science types are secretive.' He put on a thoughtful look. 'I suppose I could always ask them.'

Paul laughed. 'Yeah, like they're going to tell you!'

Jake shrugged. 'It was just a thought,' he said. Then he added hopefully, 'It still might be worth a try. They can only say no.'

'True,' agreed Paul. 'But if you ask me, you'll be banging your head against a brick wall.'

'Maybe,' said Jake. 'But, in case I feel like asking, what's the name of the lab in Aylesbury.'

'Can't remember.' Paul shrugged. 'I only remembered that it was in Aylesbury because I used to go out with a woman who lived near there.'

Jake's spirits sank as he heard Paul's words. He needed to find out where this lab was, but as soon as he started poking around asking questions about the lab, Gareth would hear about it, and he'd be exposed again. In danger.

'It's in the file,' said Paul.

Jake let the words sink in.

'The file?' he repeated.

Paul nodded. 'The incident file. They needed to explain to the press what had happened, so they told them the canister had been dug up and taken for examination by the Chemical Research Department – or whatever it's called – at Aylesbury. You know what these media people are like – unless they get some concrete information thrown at them they start ferreting around, digging their noses into all sorts of places where the government doesn't want them poking.'

The name and address of the lab at Aylesbury was in the file! thought Jake with a sense of elation. Why hadn't he thought of that before? It would have saved him doing all this cloak and dagger stuff with Paul to try to winkle out the address.

'Anyway,' said Jake, 'I suppose I'd better get on with some work, otherwise people will think I just stand around all day talking.'

'Of course you do.' Paul grinned. 'That's what we all do. We're press officers.'

Jake left it for a couple of hours before he went down to archives to look at the file. He didn't want to rouse any suspicions by going straight there. And he wanted to make sure he had more than one topic to check on, nice innocuous ones that wouldn't set off any alarm bells.

By eleven o'clock, he had a short list of topics he needed to check: the importance of vitamin B in the battle against Alzheimer's disease ('What sorts of foods contain vitamin B?'); the differing levels of radon gas in the various regions of the UK ('For a story about building regulations.'); the problems with accurately forecasting the weather – a guaranteed and unquestionable topic that arose almost on a daily basis; and – finally, 'and just out of curiosity' – the file on the incident that happened out in Bedfordshire with the toxic gas. Just to make sure all the t's were crossed and the i's dotted in his report. Nothing in depth, just the press report would do.

Jake's hands trembled as he opened the file. Would the information about where this so-called 'canister' had been taken really be in there? Or would he have to dig deeper? Start asking for more classified files, and so have Gareth breathing down his neck again.

No! It was there!

Jake felt excitement pulsing through him as he saw the words: *Canister taken for examination to Hadley Park Research Establishment, Stone, near Aylesbury.*

He'd located it!

# Chapter 11

At lunchtime, while Jake headed for a nearby sandwich bar to get himself some lunch, he took the opportunity to phone Lauren.

'Got it!' he said.

'Don't say any more!' warned Lauren.

'We need to meet,' said Jake.

'OK,' agreed Lauren. 'After work. Where we met last time.'

Jake frowned, puzzled. He wasn't very good at this. Did she mean where they'd last met together, which was the cafeteria outside the British Library? Or did she mean when he'd met her and Parsons, which was the South Bank?

'When you say "last time" . . . ?' he enquired.

'Oh, for heaven's sake, Jake!' groaned Lauren impatiently. 'The van!'

She hung up.

Of course, thought Jake, mentally kicking himself: Robert's van; noisy enough to stop any long-range microphones picking up conversations inside it. But then the opposition, whoever they were, might well have discovered the vehicle by now. In which case, they could well have fixed hidden microphones to it.

But then, reflected Jake, it really was a *very* noisy van, and it would have to be some supersonic microphone that could survive it.

Seven o'clock that evening found Jake, Lauren and Parsons sitting once more inside the back of Robert's van, while Robert sat in the front and ran the engine. This time he didn't even bother taking them for a run, just sat there revving the engine.

'Won't he upset the neighbours?' asked Jake, concerned.

'He can't stand his neighbours,' said Lauren. 'He keeps hoping they'll move so he can buy their house and knock the two into one. My guess is revving his engine like this fits into his plan.'

Jake shrugged. So long as they didn't all get carbon monoxide poisoning from the stationary vehicle.

'So, what have you found out?' asked Lauren.

Jake couldn't help giving her and Parsons a smug smile.

'I've discovered where they took the book,' he said.

'What?!' exclaimed Lauren.

'Where?' asked Parsons.

'A place called Hadley Park Research Establishment. It's at a village called Stone, near Aylesbury.'

'You're sure?' asked Parsons.

'Pretty sure,' said Jake.

He told them what he'd heard from Paul Evans, about the supposed canister being taken to the research establishment.

'There was no canister,' he said. 'But there was the book. And the man who turned into that . . . thing.'

Lauren and Carl exchanged thoughtful looks.

'It could be there,' said Parsons. 'After all, it had to have been taken somewhere. And it would need to be somewhere safe, where they could monitor it.'

Lauren nodded. 'We need to find out about this place.' She turned to Jake and asked, 'Can you ask about it at work? After all, it's part of your department.'

'Last time I tried that I nearly got pushed under a tube train,' Jake pointed out. 'Anyway, it'll be easier to Google it. Everything there is to know about everything is on the internet.'

'Yes, but if they're watching us, they could be hacked into our computers,' pointed out Parsons. 'Every time we do a search, they'll be checking on what we're looking for.'

Jake groaned. 'Modern technology. Nothing's secret any more! We can't do anything without them knowing what we're up to!'

'No, but someone can,' said Parsons thoughtfully. 'I've got a cousin who's a computer whizz.'

'Does this cousin have a name?' asked Lauren.

'Joe,' said Parsons. 'Still at school, but an absolute computer genius. If we want anything done without anything anyone knowing, Joe's our key.'

Great, thought Jake sourly. Some paranoid schoolboy computer geek who lives on junk food and thinks the world is involved in some giant conspiracy against him.

They left Robert still revving the engine of his van purely to annoy his neighbours, and set off for Hackney. At least we're heading back to my side of town, thought Jake. He always felt more comfortable in the part of London he lived in and knew. At least, he *had* felt more comfortable before all this business began. Now he didn't feel comfortable anywhere.

Parsons's cousin lived with his single mother on a large estate. As they walked through the estate, Jake was aware of gangs of youths on bikes and skateboards watching them as they hung around in groups by dilapidated garages.

'We should have got a taxi,' he muttered.

Parsons shrugged.

'They won't harm you,' he said. 'They're just check-ing you out, seeing if you're a threat.' He gave a wry sigh. 'Or a victim. Those are the two types who suffer here. Threats from outside, and victims. Just make sure you don't look like either.'

'How do I do that?' asked Jake.

Parsons shrugged again.

'I don't know,' he said. 'I've never thought about it.'

I think too much, that's my trouble, thought Jake ruefully. I think and worry. I see danger everywhere, especially lately. I never used to be like this! Then he amended that. Yes, I did, he thought. He'd always been worried about things. Being mugged or murdered. Being buried alive. Falling to his death from a tall building. In fact, there hadn't been much that hadn't kept Jake in an almost perpetual state of anxiety. Until Lauren came along and changed his life. Brought sunshine and happiness into it. And then he'd messed it up, and she'd left, and the misery and gloom and fears had come back again.

They reached a high-rise block of flats.

'This is it,' said Parsons. 'Twelfth floor.'

Oh God, not the lifts, thought Jake. Lifts always stank of urine, and broke down.

'Shall we take the stairs?' he said.

Parsons nodded.

'I was going to suggest that, if you two didn't mind,' he said.

Lauren looked up at the towering block.

'Fine by me, if it's fine by you two.' She shrugged.

By the time they reached the tenth floor, Jake was exhausted. His legs and back ached and he was so out of breath he felt he might well need oxygen. Lauren noticed he was lagging behind and turned back. 'Are you OK, Jake?' she asked.

Jake forced a smile.

'Fine,' he managed to splutter out. 'I don't think I'm as fit as I used to be.'

'You're spending too much time at a desk,' said Lauren. 'You need to get out more.'

'I will,' Jake promised.

As they mounted the stairs for the last two flights, he felt happier. That had been a genuine look of concern for him on Lauren's face.

They reached the twelfth floor and walked to a flat midway along the balcony.

'Here we are,' said Parsons. He rang the doorbell. The door opened just a little and a harassed-looking woman peered out at them through the crack. She relaxed when she saw who it was.

'Carl!' she said.

'Hello, Aunt Midge.' Parsons smiled. 'I phoned Joe and said I'd be over.'

Aunt Midge looked at Jake and Lauren standing beside him, and her face became worried again. She cast a nervous look inside the flat, and then asked in an urgent whisper, 'This isn't one of those interventions, is it? Because really Joe is . . .'

'No, no,' Parsons assured her with a laugh. 'It really is just a call. We've got something to ask Joe.'

'OK,' said the woman, and she opened the door wider to let them in. As Jake and Lauren followed Parsons along the corridor, she called after them plaintively, 'But if you can get Joe to do something else other than be stuck at that computer . . .'

'I'll try, Aunt Midge,' called back Parsons.

Oh God, thought Jake, I was right. We're about to enter the stinking bedroom of some overweight greasy teen computer nerd. It'll be strewn with empty pizza boxes and burger wrappers, and posters of Darth Vader on the walls, and the stench of rotting food and teenage-boy hormones will peel the linings off my nostrils.

He let Lauren follow Parsons first into the room. As he expected, it was dark. The curtains were closed. And there was a figure hunched over a keyboard at a small table near the bed, barely illuminated by the glow from the screen.

'Hi, Joe,' Parsons said cheerfully.

As Jake's eyes grew accustomed to the gloom, he saw that the boy was actually wearing a hood concealing his head.

Grief, groaned Jake inwardly: wearing a hoodie indoors. This cousin of Parsons is in a worse state than I thought.

Strangely, though, there were no empty pizza boxes or food wrappers. Not even a crisp packet. In fact, the room was surprisingly neat.

The boy turned round and surveyed the visitors from beneath his hood.

'Three of you?' he said. 'What is this? Some kind of convention?'

The boy's voice was surprisingly light for a teenager. He's obviously a lot younger than I thought, mused Jake.

'No, we want your help,' said Parsons. 'We need you to do a search for us.'

The boy studied them. Now Jake could see that he had a really thin face beneath his hoodie, and no weight at all on his body. OK, so not the stereotypical overweight computer nerd.

'Why can't you do it?' asked Joe.

'Because we need a machine that isn't being spied on,' said Parsons. He gestured at Jake and Lauren. 'They're under surveillance, which makes me think I could be, too.'

Jake saw the boy's eyes light up in his pale face at this and he pulled back his hood to get a better look at them. As he did so, Jake realised with a shock that he wasn't a boy. He was a girl of about fourteen or fifteen. So, not 'Joe' but 'Jo'!

'Under surveillance from who?' asked Jo, obviously intrigued.

'The government,' said Jake.

'Cool.' Jo smiled. 'Why?'

'Can we ask the questions later?' asked Parsons. 'While you're doing the searches.'

'Sure.' Jo nodded. 'What are we looking for.'

'A place called Hadley Park Research Establishment,' Jake told her. 'It's in a village called Stone, near Aylesbury.'

Jo's nimble fingers began to flit over the keyboard of her laptop. As she typed, she asked, 'What's it do?'

'We're not sure,' said Parsons. 'That's what we're hoping you'll find out for us.'

On the screen appeared a list of links, with brief comments beneath.

'It's some kind of secret science place,' murmured Jo. 'Does that sound right?'

'Yes,' said Lauren.

Jo continued scrolling down the screen.

'Hey, aliens!' she said, pleased. 'Really cool!'

'Aliens?' repeated Jake, puzzled.

'Yeah. That's just one of the things they reckon is going on here. There's the usual stuff. The Animal Rights people accuse it of experimenting on animals.

One of those Liberty-type outfits reckons it's keeping prisoners there to experiment on. But this one looks the coolest!'

'Aren't you worried about the government spying on you through your computer?' asked Jake.

Jo laughed. 'No,' she said. 'I've got my own firewalls set up. No one can break through them.' She chuckled. 'And believe me, people have tried!'

She connected to a link, and up came a site declaring itself 'AlienWatch'. It was a series of postings. Jo scrolled down until she came to the one she was looking for.

'There!' she said, and moved her chair back so they could all read the words on the posting.

'Stardate 5 March. Action at Hadley Park. Today, armed soldiers and people in hazard suits rushed into HPRE, protecting two ambulances. There'd been reports of big discs in the sky. Coincidence? More likely Roswell, UK. Do we get to see the alien autopsies from the crash site this time, or will this be yet another cover-up!'

'Roswell?' asked Jake, puzzled.

Jo turned to him and curled her lip in a sneer. She turned to Parsons. 'He doesn't know about Roswell?' she said, her tone very disapproving.

'Roswell, New Mexico,' said Lauren. 'Site of a UFO crash in 1947. The bodies were taken for autopsy and the whole thing was kept secret. Still *is* a secret, officially.'

Jo looked at Lauren admiringly.

'Hey, you're cool!' she said.

Lauren smiled at her. 'I can't do cool things like you're doing,' she complimented Jo back.

Suddenly a realisation hit Jake.

'March the fifth!' he burst out. 'That's it!'

The others looked at him, surprised.

'What is?'

'The day of the dig,' he said. 'The day they dug that thing up and the man turned into that . . . thing.' He pointed at the screen. '*That's* what they took into Hadley Park. The book and the man. Or, at least, his remains.'

'His remains?' echoed Jo, a note of shock in her voice.

The other three exchanged looks, then Jake said, 'We have to tell her.'

'I'm not sure,' said Parsons doubtfully. 'We don't want to drag her into this.'

'You already have,' Jo pointed out.

'Yes, but only so far,' said Parsons carefully. 'It's not right to put you into a . . . ' He hesitated, then said carefully, 'A difficult position.'

'What do you mean, difficult?' demanded Jo.

'Well . . .' began Parsons.

94

'He means dangerous,' cut in Lauren. 'They've already broken into my place and stolen my laptop and the evidence I had.'

'And they tried to kill me,' said Jake. 'They tried to push me under a train.'

Jo now looked at Jake with awe in her eyes.

'Cool!'

Parsons shook his head.

'No, it's not cool,' he said firmly. 'I was wrong to come here with this. And especially wrong to bring these two.'

'Well, you've already done it.' Jo shrugged. 'So you might as well tell me the rest.'

'No,' repeated Parsons, his tone even firmer. 'We can leave now, and even if anybody has been watching, we won't have been here long enough for them to get suspicious.'

'Maybe Jo can suggest someone else,' said Jake. 'Someone who won't mind being at risk. Maybe someone older?'

He'd said the wrong thing.

'I'm sixteen, rivet-head!' snapped Jo. 'I can do loads of things legally. And you can talk – you don't even look like you're old enough to shave!'

'This isn't getting us anywhere,' said Lauren. She sighed. 'I'm sorry, Jo, but I think Jake and Carl are right. This could be dangerous. It's all right for us . . .'

'Why?' demanded Jo angrily.

'Because we're older,' said Lauren.

Jo glared at her.

'Queen Victoria took over the throne when she was just eighteen. And she became ruler of over half the world,' she snapped. 'And then there was that boy of sixteen who sailed round the world single-handed. So don't talk to me about being too young for this.'

Jake nodded. 'She's got a point,' he said.

Jo added, 'And there's something at this Hadley place you want, right?'

'Yes,' nodded Jake. 'At least, we think there is.'

'Well, you're going to need me if you want to get inside the place.'

Jake looked at Jo, really taken aback. Was this girl some kind of burglar?

Jo had turned back to her keyboard and her fingers moved at speed over it. And then, on the screen, appeared an architect's drawing: a building plan.

'There!' said Jo triumphantly. 'The floor plan of Hadley Park.'

Jake's mouth dropped open. 'How did you do that?' he asked.

'Easy.' Jo shrugged. 'Every building in the country has to register their plans with their local authority. Once you know the address of the place you're looking for, and what local council it comes under, the rest is easy.' She gave a mischievous grin. 'You want the plans for Buckingham Palace?' she asked.

Jake looked at Parsons, stunned.

'Your cousin is a security risk!' he said.

'Easy!' smirked Jo. She flicked the keys, and the architect's plan on the screen was replaced by another, and another, and another.

'We need to find out where they'll have likely stashed this thing,' she muttered. 'It's dangerous, right? That's why the hazard suits.'

'Yes,' said Jake.

Jo flicked a key, and the architect's plans vanished and the list of links about Hadley Park came up again.

'Let's see what the chatter says,' she muttered. Rapidly, she scrolled down, then went to another page, and another, then another.

'It looks like Block C is where all the security stuff happens,' she announced. 'According to the whispers and gossip on these blogs and posts, there are weird goings-on in Block C. So I'll put my money on whatever you're looking for being stashed there.'

She hit a key, and the architect's plans for Hadley Park Research Establishment came upon again. She scrolled across the drawings on the screen, and then stopped, and they saw the diagram of a small block sub-divided into rooms.

'Block C.' Jo smiled. 'That's where it is.'

'Hmm,' said Jake doubtfully. 'It's all very well knowing that's where the book is, but how do we get in?'

'A *book*?!' Jo's voice rose in disbelief. 'This is about a *book*!'

'Not just any book,' said Lauren. 'This is a book the government doesn't want anyone to know about.'

'Government secrets?' asked Jo.

'In a way,' said Parsons, shooting a guarded look at both Lauren and Jake. We don't need to tell her about the Order of Malichea, he seemed to be saying. Let's keep this simple.

Jake nodded.

'Like I was saying, there's going to be all sorts of security,' he said. 'Armed guards. Dogs.'

'Electronic keypads on the doors.' Parsons nodded.

'They won't be a problem,' said Jo. 'I'll disable them.'

'How?' asked Jake.

'I hack into their security system and override the locks on Block C, of course,' said Jo. 'Though it's best to do it only for a short while. If I unlock all the doors too soon, there's a chance it'll be spotted. You know, someone walking around checking.'

'So we'd need to fix an agreed time,' said Lauren.

'Right.' Jo nodded. 'If you're standing ready by the door at, say, eleven thirty, I'll make sure the locks are off.' She flicked more keys and a series of schematic diagrams appeared on the screen, which she studied. 'Though you won't want the locks switched off for too long. There's bound to be a fail-safe cut-in that sets an alarm off if they're turned off for a certain length of time. There usually is with this sort of security system.'

Jake looked at Jo as she worked, stunned. This girl was just sixteen years old, and yet she could hack into a top-security government research lab and open all the locks on the doors just by pressing a few computer keys! It was incredible!

Then an awful thought hit him.

'Hang on,' he said, concerned. 'How do we get into the place? And how do we get to this Block C? Like I said before, there are bound to be all sorts of security systems you can't deal with just by hitting a computer. Guards. Dogs. Electrified fences.'

'I might be able to cut off the electricity to the fence,' said Jo, 'but there could be a back-up system. The only way to really do it would be to shut down the electricity supply to the whole place.'

'Which would alert the guards and raise the alarm,' pointed out Parsons.

Jo had put the plan of the research base back on the screen; this one showed the plan of the whole base, including the fences that surrounded it.

'The fence is electrified, OK.' She nodded. Then she smiled. 'But there's one thing they forgot.' She highlighted an area near the fence and pressed a key. 'There,' she said.

'What are we looking at?' asked Jake, puzzled.

'Drains,' said Parsons. 'Storm drains.'

Jo nodded. 'Right,' she said. 'A place like this can't afford to be flooded. There's a storm drain runs right across the base, and it comes out into a culvert just outside the fence . . . here.'

Jake and the others peered closer at the screen. Yes, there was a culvert of some sort marked on the plan. Jo moved the plan on the screen.

'It looks like there's a manhole from the drain just near the main building.'

'How far is it from there to Block C?' asked Lauren.

'According to the scale on the plan, about a hundred metres,' said Parsons thoughtfully.

'We can do that,' nodded Lauren.

Jake looked at her, shocked.

'A hundred metres? With armed guards and dogs?'

'We don't know there are armed guards and dogs,' pointed out Lauren.

'Yes, we do,' said Jo, studying the screen. 'I've hacked into their guard roster.'

Lauren shrugged. 'OK, so we run,' she said. 'It's not that far. Usain Bolt can run that distance in under ten seconds.'

'We are *not* Usain Bolt,' countered Jake.

'When are you going in?' asked Jo.

We're not, thought Jake. Not without doing a lot of serious checking out this place first.

'Tonight,' said Lauren.

Jake stared at her.

'Tonight?' he echoed.

'The sooner the better,' she said. 'They might move the book somewhere else.'

'OK,' said Jo. 'I'll have the alarm systems off and the locks undone at eleven thirty. I reckon I can give you twenty minutes before they need to be switched on again. After that, the fail-safe alarm system might cut in.'

'Will twenty minutes be enough?' asked Lauren, concerned.

'It should be,' said Parsons. 'If all goes to plan.'

No, it won't! Jake wanted to yell out loud. We'll get caught! We'll get put in jail for life! The guard dogs will tear us to pieces!

'Is that all right with you, Jake?' asked Lauren.

Jake did his best to appear casual.

'OK by me,' he said.

'Right, I think we'd better go and make our arrangements,' said Parsons. 'We've got some serious planning to do.' He looked at Jo, concerned. 'If you have any doubts about doing this, Jo, just let me know. We can always try and come up with something else.'

Yes, please, begged Jake. Say you have doubts, Jo!

Instead, Jo shrugged.

'No,' she said. 'It should be fun.'

Fun, groaned Jake to himself. That's not the word I'd use to describe it.

'OK.' Parsons nodded. 'We'll leave you to it.' He was just about to head for the door of Jo's room, when he stopped and gave her an apologetic, awkward smile. 'By the way, I told your mum I'd have a word with you,' he said.

'Yeah?' asked Jo.

'She thinks you ought to get out more. And I agree with her.'

Jo looked at him with distaste.

'Out*side*?' she asked.

'Yes,' Parsons said. 'It's healthy out there.'

'There are muggers, rapists and murderers out there,' said Jo. 'How can you call that healthy?'

# Chapter 12

Their next stop was a small block of flats in Kentish Town. We're doing a complete tour of London this evening, reflected Jake. Anyone who's following us is certainly earning their money. Not that they'd spotted anyone following them, but then these people would be professionals.

'This is where Carl lives,' Lauren told Jake as they followed Parsons into the courtyard of the small block and then across to a row of garages.

Parsons had unlocked one of the garages and lifted up the door. Inside was a black Mini, and on hooks and shelves on the walls hung tools and equipment: battery chargers, tyre levers, tool boxes, saws; all tidily arranged and even with labels on the shelves detailing the various items.

'Wow!' said Jake, impressed. 'You're Mr Handyman. And catalogued!'

'I take care of things,' agreed Parsons. 'Not only does it make running a car cheaper, I like to understand how things work.' He patted the Mini. 'This is what we'll go in tonight.'

Jake looked at the car doubtfully.

'These things are bigger inside than you think,' said Parsons, clearly reading Jake's mind. 'And we don't want some huge vehicle that'll draw attention to us.'

Yes, we do, thought Jake. We want a big enough vehicle that will mean the police will get suspicious when we park near the base and tell us to go away. He'd agreed to go on this stupid mission because he knew how much it meant to Lauren, but he broke out in a cold sweat when he thought of what they would actually be *doing*. Breaking into a high-security research establishment. People got shot for doing that, especially with all the fears about terrorists.

Parsons reached up to a hook and took down a heavy-looking double-handed tool.

'You're going to need these. Bolt cutters.'

'What for?' asked Jake. 'Jo said she'd have the locks open.'

'Yes, but you're going to have to get into the drain from the culvert to get inside the base. The drain could have a metal grille over it. If it's made of thick iron bars, you won't be able to cut through it without attracting attention. Not quickly, anyway. But if it's just a thick wire grille, those will do.'

Please let the drain have a heavy metal grille over it, prayed Jake. Then we'll have to pack up and leave.

'You'll also need some kind of mask,' added Parsons as he put the bolt cutters and other tools in the boot of the car. 'To stop you being identified on the CCTV.'

Jake looked at Parsons suspiciously.

'Why do I get the impression you've done this sort of thing before?' he asked.

'Anti-nuclear activities,' said Parsons. 'Sabotaging drilling rigs on possible waste sites, that sort of thing. I've got a couple of balaclava helmets indoors you can use, if you haven't got your own.'

No way am I going to put my head inside one of Parsons's sweaty stinky balaclavas, vowed Jake to himself.

'That's all right,' he said. 'I've got a ski mask at home.'

Lauren looked at him, surprised.

'Why on earth do you have one of those?' she asked.

'If you must know, after we broke up I decided to go and do something I'd never done before to make me feel better,' admitted Jake. 'I decided to go skiing.'

'Where did you go?'

Jake looked uncomfortable.

'Actually, I never went. I got the ski mask and the gloves, and then realised I couldn't afford it. But one day I will!'

'I don't think we've got time to go to Jake's place and get his ski mask,' said Parsons. He tapped his watch. 'It's late already, and we have to get to Stone by eleven at the latest if you're going to be waiting by the doors of Block C at eleven thirty.'

'Then we'll use your balaclavas,' announced Lauren.

It was nearly eleven o'clock as they left the ring road around Aylesbury and headed on the road to Stone. Parsons and Lauren were in the front of the Mini, and Jake was crammed in the back. He reflected ruefully that a Mini was large enough inside to sit comfortably, if you were in the front. The back was fine if you were one of the Seven Dwarfs, but for someone tall like Jake, he'd had to fold himself up to get in. It had also just begun to rain.

Great, thought Jake. We're going to be crawling along a drain, with water pouring through.

The rain got heavier as the lights above the high wire fence of Hadley Park Research Establishment came into view. The place was lit up like a Christmas tree. And it looked huge; the fence and the harsh lights went on for about a quarter of a mile along the road. Parsons turned left, taking a narrow side road that bordered the edge of the base. The fence and lights continued down this road, but there were also trees and small wooded areas on the other side. Parsons continued for a further hundred metres, pulled into a gap between two trees, and drove over the bumpy uneven ground into a small clearing.

'How did you know this place was here?' asked Jake.

'I came to Aylesbury years ago to visit an aunt, and we came out here for a drink in the village pub. Then we came to this spot to pick blackberries.'

'Lucky for us,' said Lauren.

Or is it? thought Jake. It was all too much of a coincidence, as far as he was concerned. He was tempted to dig deeper, ask Parsons the name of this supposed aunt, but he thought that might upset Lauren.

'One last thing,' said Parsons. 'Leave any wallets, or anything with any identification of any sort, in the car. If you drop anything while you're in there, all this is a waste of time; they'll know who you are anyway and will come and pick you up.'

The professional action man, thought Jake grimly as he took out his wallet and other bits of paper from his pockets and dumped them on the back seat. He had to admit, the fact that Parsons seemed to be experienced in this sort of covert activity made Jake feel even more jealous of him.

They got out of the car and Parsons pointed through the bushes that shielded them from the road and the base.

'According to the plan Jo pulled up, the culvert should be just along there. I'll wait for you here.'

'What will you do if someone finds you?' asked Lauren.

'Hopefully this rain will keep people indoors,' replied Parsons. 'But if I am confronted by anyone, I will reluctantly admit that I am having an affair with a local married woman, and I'm meeting her here.'

'I can't see them believing that,' snorted Jake.

'Why not?' asked Parsons. 'I bet you it happens a lot around here, illicit meetings in wooded places like this, off the beaten track.'

Lauren checked her watch.

'We need to hurry,' she said. 'It's ten past eleven. We've only got twenty minutes before Jo opens the locks.'

*If* she opens the locks, thought Jake. He felt sick. This whole escapade was a foolish nightmare. There were so many things that could go wrong: they wouldn't be able to get into the drain. If they did, they'd get stuck and drown because of this rain. Even if they did manage to get inside, they'd be caught by security guards or dogs. At the thought of a vicious-toothed slavering Alsatian attacking him, Jake felt himself go weak. And, even if they made it to this Block C, what were the chances that Parsons's odd cousin would have actually been able to hack into the security system and disable the locks?

It was just some weird fantasy on her behalf, pretending to be some cyber-terrorist. Jo was playing games. But this was real. If they were caught – and the chances were they would be caught – then jail was an absolute certainty. Providing they weren't shot dead first. No, this was a *bad* idea. A *very* bad idea.

'Ready, Jake?' asked Lauren.

And she gave him a smile. It was the smile that did it. Jake nodded.

'Ready,' he said.

# Chapter 13

Jake and Lauren left the cover of the small copse and hurried across the narrow road towards the high wire fence. A ditch ran between the road and the fence.

'D'you reckon this'll take us to the culvert?' asked Lauren.

'Only one way to find out,' said Jake.

He pulled the balaclava over his head, and then slid down into the ditch. Lauren followed him. The ditch was full of brambles, and Jake was glad they were completely encased in clothes, with thick gloves and the balaclava helmets, or the brambles would have torn their skin to ribbons. The heavy rain was starting to fill the ditch now, though, making the weeds and mud in it slippery underfoot. They moved off. All the while Jake's senses were on alert for the sound of an alarm from the base, or a shout that showed they'd been spotted.

Aware of the time limit on them, they moved swiftly along the ditch. Finally Jake spotted the concrete of the culvert, partly overgrown by weeds and nettles. They followed the culvert until they came to the drain outlet.

'It's good!' whispered Lauren, relief in her voice.

Jake saw what she meant: there was just a grille made of wire, partly hidden behind nettles. Obviously no one bothered to check the drain was cleared.

Lauren hurried to the wire grille, took hold of it, and pulled at it. It moved slightly, but held.

'Bolt cutters?' whispered Lauren.

Jake passed her the cutters. She set to work, cutting through the wires of the grille.

Jake sneaked a look at his watch. 11.17. They had thirteen minutes. He tried to recall the plan of the drain on Jo's computer screen, and how it related to the base, and particularly Block C. Block C was near the third manhole from the drain entrance; he was fairly sure of that.

Lauren cut through the last of the wires and heaved on the grille, bending it down. The entrance to the drain was open!

She turned to him and gave him a thumbs-up. He couldn't see her face beneath the balaclava, but he guessed she was smiling. So far so good.

Lauren slid into the drain. Once inside, she produced a small torch and shone it along it. As Jake joined her inside the drain entrance he looked past her and saw that the drain ahead was clear. A trickle of water ran down in their direction, but not enough to stop them. He checked his watch again. 11.22. Eight minutes.

Lauren was already sliding further in and upwards through the narrow drain, hauling herself along with her clawed gloved fingers and her knees. Jake followed close behind her, his face almost touching the backs of her legs. Every now and then he was aware of the torch beam being aimed at the top of the drain-tunnel, and then Lauren moved on again. Finally, she stopped. She gestured upwards.

Jake looked at where the beam of torchlight was pointing at a manhole cover. Lauren rolled on to her back and reached up, and began pushing at the metal cover. For a second Jake thought it was stuck fast, but then he saw it move slightly, and suddenly it was clear. Heavy rain began to pour down over them, and on down the tunnel past them.

Lauren pushed herself up, and then out of the drain. Jake followed her, wriggling himself into a position from where he could stand, and then he used the sides of the open manhole to lever himself up.

The rain was certainly heavier now. He slid the manhole cover almost back into place, taking care to leave an edge sticking up. The last thing they'd need would be to be running from fast-closing pursuers and finding the manhole cover stuck.

They'd come up just behind a wooden hut. Lauren sidled carefully towards the edge of the hut, and peered round. She gave Jake a thumbs-up again, and then headed across a patch of open ground towards a single-storey concrete building. As Jake hurried after her, he could see the words 'Block C' in huge letters painted on the building's wall. He slipped on the wet grass as he ran and nearly lost his balance, but managed to recover himself. Thank heaven for this rain, he thought. It would reduce visibility, help them avoid being spotted.

He joined Lauren at the door to the building. Fortunately, it was in shadow, away from the harsh lights of the fence. Here we go, he thought.

Lauren reached for the door handle and looked at Jake, questioningly. Was he ready?

He nodded and gave her a thumbs-up. Let's do it.

Lauren tried to push the handle down, but nothing happened. The handle stayed locked straight in the same position. Lauren tried again, but once more the door handle stayed firmly locked.

'She said she'd have it open!' burst out Jake, horrified.

Lauren checked her watch.

'It's eleven twenty-nine,' she said. 'Jo said eleven thirty.'

But Jake could hear the anxiety in her voice, and knew that she was as scared as he was.

They both kept their eyes on the time, watching as the seconds passed. Then, at precisely 11.30, they heard a click from the door. Lauren tried pushing the handle down again. This time it swung down.

'Let's hope she's cut off the alarms as well,' said Lauren nervously.

'We're about to find out,' whispered Jake. He felt a panic in him so bad he could barely breathe. He pulled at the door. It opened. No alarm went off.

'Maybe it's a silent alarm,' he said. 'It goes off at their control room.'

'If that's the case, it's too late now to change it,' said Lauren. 'Jo said she'd give us twenty minutes. Let's get going.'

They slipped into the building, and then pulled the door closed after them. Let's hope we can get out, prayed Jake.

Ahead of them was a corridor, lit by banks of fluorescent lights. The building was quiet, except for the hum of electricity. Possibly a generator. As they moved carefully along the hallway, the electric hum seemed to get louder. Maybe it was a machine of some sorts. A series of doors ran along both walls, with windows in the doors so that every room could be observed from this main corridor. Low-level lighting shone through the window in every door, suggesting that no one was actually working in the building at this moment, but that stand-by lighting was in operation.

Jake checked his watch. 11.35. He tapped Lauren on the shoulder, and when she turned, he gestured at his watch. They had just fifteen minutes before the locks shut down again.

Lauren nodded and moved on, Jake close behind her. Where would the book be kept? Would it be on open show? Would it be locked away? In which case, they'd never find it in fifteen minutes.

Suddenly, a movement through one of the glass windows caught Jake's eye, and his heart almost stopped. He turned, and then froze. Inside the room something was lying on a table, and as he watched it moved slightly. He strained to see into the gloom, and became aware that the thing, whatever it was, was strapped to a table. And then he realised with horror it was a man. Not just any man, but the builder who'd been turned into a mass of vegetation at the building site. Now Jake could see the medical equipment around the table, drips and monitors, tubes and cables going into the mass of vegetation; broad leather straps holding the thing down. The thing moved again, and – as Jake's gaze travelled along the shape – the top of it turned and a pair of eyes looked directly at him, making him stumble back.

He's alive! thought Jake. And he's seen me!

A touch on his arm nearly made him collapse with fright. It was Lauren, gesturing along the corridor. He hurried after her, his nerves jangling, his throat dry. What other monstrosities were there in this building?

He caught up with Lauren as she opened a door and hurried in. She pointed, and Jake saw that on an aluminium table in the centre of the room was a glass case, and inside the glass case was a book-sized object covered in what looked like leather or oilskin. With growing excitement, Jake realised that they'd found it! They'd found the book!

Lauren was already trying to lift the glass case from its base, but it was shut tight. The lock on the glass case wasn't part of the central security system, but an old-fashioned metal lock set into the glass, with a keyhole in it.

Lauren tried to force the glass cover up, but it wouldn't budge. Jake tried with her, but even with their combined efforts the glass case remained firmly closed.

So near and yet so far, thought Jake. We've come this far, we can't go without it. He looked at his watch. 11.46. Four minutes before the place went into lock-down. It would take them two minutes to get back to the exit door. If they didn't leave here soon, they'd be trapped.

Jake cast his eye around the room, and saw a large stone with ornate carvings on it. They looked as if they were Celtic. It was possibly some other ancient artefact that had been brought in for examination. Jake picked up the stone and felt its heaviness. Lauren was still trying to heave the glass cover off. Jake lifted the heavy stone, and then swung it hard at the glass.

The glass shattered, and as it did the ear-splitting sound of an alarm blared out. Lauren swung round, shocked, but Jake was already reaching into the shattered glass cabinet and snatching up the book.

Let's hope that alarm hasn't brought the security system back in! he prayed urgently. He ran to the door and tugged at it, and it opened. So far so good; but the alarm was still sounding out, the noise filling their heads.

They ran down the corridor and reached the exit door. As they pushed it open, they ran straight into a security guard standing just outside, and heard the vicious warning growl of a guard dog on a lead right beside him. The security guard seemed as shocked as they were, but he reached out and grabbed Lauren's balaclava and tore it off her head. Acting instinctively, Jake leapt out and swung his fist at the guard's face, connecting with his chin. The security guard stumbled back with a cry of pain, and the dog leapt at Jake. Jake felt the dog's teeth rip at his sleeve.

Acting out of survival instinct rather than with skill, Jake shoved the dazed guard into the building. The guard still had the dog's lead wrapped round his wrist, and the dog was pulled after his master; but he dragged Jake with him. Desperately, Jake slipped out of his jacket and pushed both the dog and the guard inside, then leapt back, slamming the door shut. There was a click, and Jake tried the handle again. It was locked once more!

Jake and Lauren ran back towards the manhole cover. The rain was much heavier now, the grass slippery, but they skidded to a halt beside the cover, and then slid down into the drain. The base was alive with activity now: lights coming on all over the place; sirens blaring; people shouting; dogs barking.

Jake followed Lauren into the drain and pulled the manhole cover into place. The heavy rain cascading down had turned the drain into a waterslide and they half slid, half scrambled along the narrow tunnel towards the culvert.

They forced their way through the bent wire grille, then out to the culvert, and along the ditch. Now the ditch was deep in water, and getting fuller, but they made it to where Parsons was waiting with the car.

'What happened?' he asked as they reached the Mini. 'What went wrong?'

'We'll talk as you drive,' said Lauren.

Jake and Lauren tumbled into the car, their clothes and faces soaking wet. Parsons slid behind the wheel, started the car up, and drove out of the small clearing into the narrow road. Jake noticed he was heading away from the main Aylesbury road.

'I'm using a different route, off the main road,' said Parsons, as if reading Jake's thoughts. 'We don't want to get stopped.'

Parsons waited until they'd driven for about half a mile before he switched on the car's lights.

'So, what happened?' he asked.

'We got the book,' said Lauren triumphantly.

'You did?' said Parsons, and for the first time the usually cool and calm tone in his voice broke to show excitement. 'Incredible! Fantastic!!'

'The alarm went off,' said Jake. 'The one protecting the glass case where the book was. Jo said she'd deal with the alarms.'

'Maybe it was on a different circuit,' said Parsons defensively. 'She handled the rest of the security system OK.'

'True,' acknowledged Jake. Then he told them: 'The man who turned into that vegetation is in there.'

'What?!' exclaimed Lauren.

'In a room along from where the book was. And he's alive.'

119

'My God,' said Parsons, awed.

'We have to hide the book,' said Lauren. 'Somewhere safe, where no one will find it.'

'I'll do that,' offered Parsons.

The professional action man again, thought Jake sourly.

'After all, we know they know about you two, but so far I don't think they know about me,' Parsons added.

'Yes, makes sense.' Lauren nodded. She turned to Jake and held out her hand for the book. Jake looked down at the leather-bound package he was still gripping tightly. The book. Don't open it, he told himself, or you'll end up like that heaving mass of barely alive vegetation inside the base.

'Jake,' prompted Lauren, still holding out her hand.

I want to find out what this is, thought Jake. All this trouble, all this secrecy, and I have the answer in my hand. I want to see it. At least, the cover! See what it looks like.

Instead, he passed the book forward to Lauren, who took it and slipped it into her bag.

'At last!' she said exultantly. 'The proof!'

# Chapter 14

Parsons pulled up outside Jake's flat, and Jake went in, after they'd all promised to be in touch the next day. No, *today*, Jake corrected himself. It was 2 a.m. as he entered his flat, soaked to the skin, aching in every muscle, and with a feeling of loss. He'd held the book in his hand, and now it was gone. He'd been close to Lauren tonight, so close, tied together by the bond of fear and adrenalin during the mission, and now she was gone, too. Gone with Parsons.

Next morning, Jake made his way to work. A few hours earlier, he thought he'd never be able to sleep: the adrenalin still pumping. But he had calmed down by the time he got in, and he'd slept, only to be dragged back into the waking world by his alarm clock at seven thirty.

He'd thought about phoning Lauren, then thought

better of it. What could they say over the phone, especially if their lines were bugged?

Today, no one tried to kill him. No one tried to push him under a tube train. His journey was uneventful. He walked into the large open-plan office and found Paul already there, engaged in an animated phone conversation.

'Yes, we are obviously sympathetic to the sincerity of their views, but at the same time we absolutely condemn the way this was done, not just the vicious attack on the security-guard staff, but putting everyone else at the establishment at risk and in fear of their lives, as well as the animals.'

'What animals?' asked Jake as Paul hung up the phone.

'Rabbits,' answered Paul.

'Rabbits?' echoed Jake, puzzled.

'You know, those cute furry things with long ears.'

'Ha ha, very funny,' said Jake sarcastically. 'I meant, in what way were they at risk? And the staff of . . . wherever.'

'Actually, it's that place in Aylesbury I was telling you about.'

'Aylesbury?'

Paul gave a weary groan.

'For heaven's sake, Jake, do I have to repeat *everything*?'

'I've just walked in,' pointed out Jake in his defence, 'and you start talking about rabbits as if I know what's going on.'

'OK.' Paul nodded. 'Well, you know that place I told you they'd taken that canister of stuff?'

Jake was about to respond with a nod and the words 'the Hadley Park Research Establishment', but he stopped himself just in time. All Paul had told him was the place was in Aylesbury. He didn't want awkward questions being asked if he told Paul he'd looked up the file.

'The place in Aylesbury,' he said.

'That's the one,' said Paul. 'Well, last night some Animal Rights campaigners broke in and released a load of rabbits.' As an afterthought, he added by way of explanation: 'Apparently they conduct tests on rabbits there.'

'What sort of tests?'

Paul shrugged.

'I don't know. Cancer. Cosmetics. Anyway, it caused a major hoo-ha, alarms going off, the local residents worried.' He grinned. 'Apparently, one of the locals thought there might be some sort of biological weapon testing going on that had gone wrong. Luckily, we were able to reassure them it was just Animal Rights freeing rabbits. And that the rabbits were perfectly healthy and absolutely *not* contaminated with anything.'

123

'How do we know it was Animal Rights campaigners?' asked Jake.

'Because they sent out a press release,' said Paul, picking up a sheet of paper from his desk and handing it to Jake.

Jake read it. The heading said 'MAAT', and beneath it the words: *Militants Against Animal Testing*. The message was simple. *We of MAAT oppose the inhumane use of animals for testing*. Then followed some statistics about the use of rabbits for testing cosmetics: how rabbits were ideal for testing harmful chemicals in cosmetics because they didn't have tear ducts to wash away the toxic substances; and how rabbits were kept tied up while new experimental brands of shampoo were poured into their eyes. The press release ended with the words: *Stop this Cruelty Now!*

Paul shook his head.

'Mad people,' he sighed.

No, *clever* people, thought Jake. There had been no freeing of rabbits from Hadley Park last night. Someone had worked very quickly to come up with this story and the press release from this so-called mythical 'MAAT', to calm the worried residents of Stone.

Just then the phone on his desk rang. He picked it up.

'Jake Wells, press office,' he said.

'Good,' said a woman's voice. 'I'm glad you're OK.'

He frowned, puzzled.

'Who is this?' he asked.

'Penny Johnson. We met at the site . . .'

The reporter! thought Jake. 'Yes, I remember,' he said.

'I wonder if we can meet and talk?' asked Johnson.

Jake hesitated. The last thing he wanted was to stir things up and arouse Gareth's suspicions. Right now, it was best that he kept a low profile. 'Well . . .' he began, reluctantly.

'Oh, don't put me off!' begged Johnson. 'Look, you're a press officer. I'm a journalist. We have to talk to one another, it's in our job descriptions.'

'Yes, but . . .'

'Can you be free in ten minutes?'

Ten minutes? She was that close! My God, was this woman stalking him?

'Well . . .' he began again, awkwardly.

'Stop saying "Well",' said Johnson. 'Leave my name at your reception desk and I'll see you there in ten minutes. If you need an official reason to see me, I've got a story I need to run past you, and you're the only one who can verify it.'

'OK,' said Jake. 'Ten minutes.'

He phoned down to the front desk and gave them Penny Johnson's name and his extension. As he hung

125

up he thought: what does she know? And why does she need to see me?

She was on time. Ten minutes later, Jake's phone rang.

'Your guest has arrived,' said reception. 'A Miss Penny Johnson.'

'Tell her I'm on my way down,' said Jake.

As he headed down to the ground floor, he wondered what story she wanted to see him about. It had to do with the dig, and whatever had been dug up. But the case had been dealt with, first by Algy, and then by Paul and others in the press office: it was a release of toxic gas, and the canister had been removed for safety to a research establishment, where it was being checked. So why had she gone to all the trouble of coming in to London from Bedfordshire, and to see him specifically?

Penny Johnson was standing by the reception desk, waiting for him.

'Hi,' he said. 'You said you had a story?'

Johnson nodded.

'Is there somewhere we can talk?' she asked.

Jake gave a rueful shrug.

'If you want to talk privately, everything upstairs is open-plan,' he apologised. He gestured towards a dark leather settee at one side of the large reception hall.

'Down here is fine,' said Johnson, and she walked to the settee, Jake following. Once they were sitting

126

down she said, 'There was a stir at Hadley Park Research Establishment last night.'

Warning bells sounded in Jake's mind. Hadley Park, he thought. This isn't about the dig, it's about the break-in. He kept his face as bland as he could.

'So I understand.' He nodded. 'Animal Rights campaigners freeing rabbits.'

'That's what the press release says.'

'Their *own* press release,' pointed out Jake.

'Interestingly enough, I can't find anyone who's ever heard of this outfit, MAAT, before.'

Jake shrugged.

'That's the way it is with subversive organisations: there are new ones springing up all the time. Most of them breaking away from bigger outfits.' He gave a chuckle. 'Like in *Life of Brian*: the Judean Liberation Front and their mortal enemies, the Liberation Front of Judea.'

'So, this is a new organisation?' she asked.

Immediately, Jake grew cautious. 'They *may* be new,' he said. 'I'd have to check with our archives.' Then he frowned. 'Anyway, I understand the research establishment where the break-in occurred is in Buckinghamshire. You work for the *Bedfordshire Times*.'

'It's just over the county border,' responded Johnson. 'At that point three counties connect: Beds, Bucks and Herts, all within the radius of a few miles. It's hard to separate them as far as news stories are concerned. People from Beds live and work in Bucks and Herts, and vice versa.'

Jake shrugged again.

'Anyway, all I can do is repeat the official line,' he said. 'Animal Rights campaigners broke in and freed some rabbits.'

'So it was nothing to do with the Order of Malichea,' she said.

Jake stared at her, momentarily stunned, a feeling of panic welling up inside him. For what seemed like an eternity, he couldn't breathe. Finally he forced his mouth into what he hoped looked like a smile and gave a chuckle.

'Look . . .' he began, doing his best to look both puzzled and amused. It didn't work. She shook her head.

'It's no good,' Johnson said. 'I saw the look in your eyes at the mention of the name. Panic. Why?'

Jake shook his head firmly.

'I wasn't panicking,' he said. 'It was just . . . surprise. The name came up recently in some research . . .'

'Nonsense,' said Johnson. She leant forward. 'I can help you,' she whispered.

'Help me what?' asked Jake, still desperately hanging on to his pretence that he hadn't got the faintest idea what she was talking about.

'A book was dug up at that site,' Johnson told him coolly. 'It was taken to Hadley Park. Last night, someone got into Hadley Park and took the book.'

Jake looked her squarely in the face.

'Where do you get all this from?' he asked. 'What book?'

'The book needs to go back to its rightful owners,' said Johnson.

Jake stared at her, bewildered.

'Its rightful owners?' he echoed.

Johnson nodded.

Jake shook his head, bewildered. Really bewildered.

'I don't understand what you're saying,' he said.

'You will,' said Johnson. She looked at her watch. 'I have to go.' She took a card from her bag and handed it to Jake. 'These are my contact numbers. You can get hold of me any time, twenty-four hours a day.' As Jake took it, she looked him firmly in the eyes and said, 'If you haven't got the book, you need to tell whoever has it that it must be returned. I can arrange that. But it must be soon. It mustn't fall into the wrong hands.'

With that she stood up, and gave him a smile.

'Call me,' she said. 'And soon.'

# Chapter 15

Jake's mind was a whirl as he headed back to the office. Johnson hadn't acted like a reporter keen for a story. She'd acted like . . . like someone who already knew what was going on. *The book needs to go back to its rightful owners*. How did she know about the book? And who were the rightful owners? The Order of Malichea? But the Order had died out hundreds of years ago.

As he walked through the door of the large office, he stopped. Gareth was standing with Paul at Paul's desk and they were looking at something on the screen of Paul's computer. To his horror, Jake realised what it was: CCTV images from a security camera just outside Block C at Hadley Park. Even through the rain he could see the words 'Block C' clearly. And two figures standing by the closed door: one of them with no jacket on, but still wearing a balaclava helmet hiding his face, and the other with no helmet and her face showing clearly on the screen. Lauren. The CCTV must have started up again as the security system and the locks were turned back on by Jo, and they'd caught Jake and Lauren. But only Lauren was in full view and recognisable.

I have to warn her, thought Jake. He took out his mobile and turned to head for the corridor, when Gareth's voice called out, 'Jake!'

Jake turned and put on a casual smile to match Gareth's beam of welcome. 'Gareth,' he responded.

'We're just watching the CCTV footage from last night's raid at Hadley Park,' said Gareth, gesturing towards the frozen image of Lauren on the screen.

'The rabbit people,' added Paul.

Jake looked at the screen.

'Do we know who it is?' he asked.

'Not yet,' said Gareth. 'We'll run her through the systems, see if anything comes up.' He turned to Jake, his face questioning. '*You* don't recognise her, do you, Jake?'

He knows! thought Jake. Frantically, Jake tried to remember if he'd ever introduced Lauren to Gareth. Maybe at some departmental do. Or had Lauren ever called at the office to meet Jake, and been spotted by Gareth?

He shook his head. 'No,' he said. He wondered if Gareth could tell he was sweating and his stomach was churning with panic. He looked at Gareth and forced a smile. Gareth's concerned expression was fixed on his face, his eyes boring into Jake's. 'Do you feel all right, Jake?'

'I'm fine, thanks,' said Jake.

Gareth shook his head.

'You say you're fine, but are you?' he asked. He sighed. 'You never went to the medico yesterday, so I hear.'

'Er . . . er,' stammered Jake.

'Remember, my instructions were to go home for a day, and then get yourself checked when you came back.'

'Er, yes,' nodded Jake. 'Sorry about that, Gareth. I'll go and see them this afternoon.'

'No, you won't,' said Gareth. 'You'll get yourself checked *now*, Jake. Don't forget, we have a duty of care for you. You *think* you're fine, but who's to say there mightn't be some vestiges of the gas still hanging around in your system.'

'OK, I'll go down and see the medicos now,' said Jake.

Gareth smiled.

'We're going to do better for you than that, Jake,' he said. 'We value you. You have a future here. And we need to invest in that future.'

132

Jake looked at him, baffled. What was he going on about? Gareth's next words sent a shock wave through him, even more than Penny Johnson's had done.

'I've fixed up for you to see one of our top men,' continued Gareth smoothly, his face expressing deep concern. 'After all, the medico here said he couldn't find anything wrong with you the other day.' Gareth shook his head disapprovingly. 'That's not good enough. You suffered harm while doing your duty, Jake. We need to get to the bottom of it, in case there could be after-effects. I've arranged for you to go and see the department's top man in Harley Street.'

He knows! thought Jake, his heart racing. He definitely knows! In some way Gareth had recognised Lauren and connected her to Jake. That, along with finding Jake earlier in the week in archives, asking about 'Sigma' and 'Malichea' . . .

Gareth was behind this. He was behind everything. He's the government man protecting the secret of Malichea, Jake told himself in a panic, and he knows it was me who took the book! Now they're going to take me to this doctor in Harley Street and shoot me up with Pentothal or some other truth drug, so I tell them where the book is. I have to get away!

Jake did his best to remain calm, fighting down the feeling of panic that threatened to overwhelm him. He looked at Paul, who appeared stunned at this surprising statement from Gareth, and also very impressed. Jake could tell what Paul was thinking: they're sending him to their top man at Harley Street! Wow, they must really care about Jake's health and well-being!

'I'm very grateful, Gareth,' said Jake. 'If you let me have the address, I'll make my way there.'

Like hell I will, thought Jake. If you think I'm walking into the arms of someone who can strap me down and inject me, you have another thing coming!

'Make your way there?' repeated Gareth, his face a picture of incredulousness. 'Good heavens, Jake, we wouldn't dream of it! Say something happened to you on the way? You fell under a bus, or under a tube train, or something.'

*It was him!* thought Jake. He arranged for me to be pushed under that train, and he's telling me! Warning me! Threatening me!

'No, no,' continued Gareth jovially. 'I've arranged a car to take you. Nothing but the best for our Jake!' He looked past Jake and his smile broadened as he announced, 'And here he is! Your driver!'

Jake turned, and his heart sank. A tall, tough-looking man stood there, dressed in a neat dark suit that barely contained his muscle-bound physique.

'Adam,' said Gareth, gesturing at Jake, 'this is Jake Wells. You're to take him to Harley Street. Dr Endicote's expecting him.'

'Right, sir,' said Adam. To Jake he said, 'The car's ready in the car park.'

'Right.' Jake nodded. He picked up his case, then he turned to Gareth. 'You're taking a lot of care about me, Gareth,' he said. 'I'm sure I'm not really worth it.'

'Nonsense!' Gareth beamed.

Jake forced another smile and followed the bulky figure of Adam out of the office and along the corridor that led to the lift to the underground car park.

Once I get in that car I'm a dead man, thought Jake.

They turned a bend in the corridor, and then another, and suddenly the lift doors were in front of them.

Act now! Jake told himself, panic rising in him.

'Hang on!' he exclaimed.

Adam turned to him, puzzled.

'I forgot something!' said Jake apologetically. 'It's in my desk. I'll be back in a second!'

Adam hesitated, then nodded. 'OK,' he said. 'I'll wait here for you.'

'Good idea.' Jake smiled. 'I always get lost going to the car park.'

Jake turned and walked away. Once he was round the bend in the corridor and out of Adam's sight, he broke into a frantic run. Get out of the building! his senses told him. Run!

He hurtled along the corridor, and past the open door of his office. Even if Gareth spotted him, Jake felt he was moving too fast for Gareth to do anything about it. What would Gareth be able to do, anyway? Shout 'Stop that man!' That was hardly Gareth's style. It would rouse all manner of suspicions in the rest of the staff.

There were no shouts as Jake rushed past his office, nor as he ran at full speed down the stairs, barely keeping his balance. He hit the marble floor of the main reception area, and then ran out through the revolving doors into the street.

I have to phone Lauren and warn her! he thought. But not just yet. Wait till I'm far enough away that I can stop moving. He'd slowed down to a walk now, so he didn't attract attention. He walked past the local sandwich bar, past the printer's and stationer's, and reached the roundabout at the end of Marsham Street. The pedestrian crossing that led over the main road, and was his route to the back streets and safety, was about a hundred metres away. He was just heading towards it, when a man stepped into his path.

'Excuse me,' said the man politely but unsmilingly. He didn't move.

'Pardon?' asked Jake, startled.

Suddenly, he was aware of someone just behind him, and then he felt something hard push into the small of his back.

'This is a gun. Don't make me use it,' murmured a voice.

# Chapter 16

A gun!

Numbly, Jake looked at the man who'd stepped in front of him. He was small but wiry. Unsmiling face, cold eyes, hair cut so short his scalp was almost shaved. He had a thin scar that ran right down the left side of his face, from his eyebrow to the corner of his mouth. A knife or a sword, thought Jake. Or a bayonet. He was wearing a casual jacket over a black T-shirt; and jeans and trainers. He looked like one of the SAS soldiers Jake had seen in documentaries, small and incredibly fit, like human pit bull terriers.

'We want the book,' said the short man.

'The one you took from Hadley Park,' came the quiet voice from behind him.

The pressure in Jake's back had eased, but Jake was still aware of the man standing very close behind him.

How did they know? Government black ops, thought Jake. They know everything. They must have caught me on camera, some secret CCTV system.

'I don't know what you're talking about,' he said.

The short man obviously expected to get this answer. His face didn't register annoyance. In fact, he didn't seem to register emotion of any sort.

'Shall I shoot him in the leg?' asked the man behind him. 'Just so he gets the message we mean business?'

'The arm would be better,' said the short man. 'We need him to be able to walk.'

The way they spoke about shooting him was so casual, so matter-of-fact, it sent a wave of terror surging through Jake. They're going to kill me, he thought. They'll torture me to get what they want; and then they'll kill me.

'You can't shoot me!' he protested. 'People will come running!'

The short man gave a weary sigh.

'It's fitted with a silencer, dummy,' he said in exasperation. 'We'll just take you somewhere.'

'We'll have come to your rescue after you've injured your arm in the street,' whispered the man behind him. 'Two friends looking after another.'

'Or you can save yourself a lot of pain and just hand over the book,' said the short wiry man.

Jake thought quickly. 'OK,' he nodded, 'it's in my office.' And he gestured along the street back towards the Department of Science building.

These men aren't from Gareth, he thought. Unless Gareth was playing a double game and Adam's job had been to frighten Jake into running out of the building and into the clutches of these two. But that didn't make sense. Adam had Jake trapped inside the building. He had a car waiting to deliver Jake to Dr Endicote, where he would undoubtedly be questioned. The way they answer this will tell me whether the men are also working for Gareth. If they think I'm able to just walk back into that building, they're not connected with Gareth. In which case, who are they working for?

The short wiry man hesitated.

He's thinking about it, thought Jake. And if they do let me go back inside the building to get the book, I'll find somewhere to hide and then get out another way. Providing Adam and Gareth aren't waiting for me, of course.

'OK,' said the short man. 'Phone your pal in the office and get him to bring it out.'

Jake stared back at him, dumb-struck.

'What?' he asked.

'You heard,' said the man. 'Take out your phone and call him. Tell him to bring the book out.'

'I don't have a pal in the office,' said Jake desperately.

'Yes, you do,' said the man. 'His name's Evans. Paul Evans.'

How do they know that? thought Jake. 'I don't know his number,' he flailed.

The short man gave a snort of disbelief.

'Oh, come on!' he sneered.

'I don't!' protested Jake. 'I never call him on the phone! He sits next to me!'

'He's faking,' said the man behind him. 'Wasting our time. I'll shoot him.'

'No!' blurted out Jake desperately. What could he do? He didn't have the book. Parsons had the book. Or, he *had* had the book. He could have put it somewhere safe by now. He gulped. 'I don't have his extension number on my mobile,' he said.

'That's no problem,' said the short man. 'Phone the main switchboard and give them his name. They'll put you through.'

Jake hesitated, looking about him. He was trapped. Everything else was going on normally around him: people coming in and out of the sandwich bar; traffic passing by; people going about their daily business, and in the centre of it, Jake was trapped between two SAS black ops soldiers with a silenced gun aimed at him. These men would have no pity for him, no sympathy. They were here to do a job: get the book off him. And they'd get it, even if it meant tearing out his fingernails, breaking his arms and legs, electrocuting him and burning him. They wanted the book.

With trembling fingers, he pulled out his mobile. He looked at it, then gulped. 'It's low on charge.'

'No problem,' said the short man. He reached into his pocket and pulled out a mobile phone. 'This one is fully charged.' He handed it to Jake, his face set in a grim expression. 'Dial,' he said firmly.

Jake gulped. He tapped in the first digit, and then suddenly threw the mobile into the doorway of a nearby shop, and at the same time ran out into the road, hurling himself in front of a car.

The car slammed on its brakes, tyres squealing in protest, and there was the horrifying sound of metal crashing into metal as the car following behind ran into the back of it; then the car behind that running into the back of the second car.

Horns blared, and the door of the first car was thrust open. A middle-aged man got out, his face twisted in fury. He reached out and grabbed hold of Jake by his jacket with both hands and began to bang him against the bonnet of the car.

'My no-claims bonus!' he roared, and then began punching Jake.

'Sorry! Sorry!' burbled Jake, putting up his arms in front of him, doing his best to defend himself.

Other people had arrived on the scene now: passers-by, tourists, drivers from some of the other cars that had pulled up on the roundabout, and the figure of a policeman.

'Stop that!' ordered the policeman, and the angry man reluctantly stopped punching Jake.

Jake shot a glance towards the pavement. The short wiry man had disappeared. He guessed his accomplice had also gone, but only for the moment. He was sure they were somewhere near, watching, and they'd be back.

# Chapter 17

Jake sat on the hard wooden chair in the interview room at the police station. He'd just given his statement to the uniformed police constable about what had happened: being threatened by the two men, and running into the road to escape them. It was obvious to Jake that the constable hadn't wanted to come all the way back to the station and take his statement. The constable had hoped this would be just a simple matter, with Jake being cautioned (or possibly charged) for causing an accident at the scene. One crime committed, one crime solved. A box ticked. 100% crime-solving success rate.

Instead of which, Jake had insisted he'd been the victim of a potentially deadly assault, and equally firmly insisted on being taken to the nearest police station to give his statement.

From Jake's point of view, it had been a strategy to ensure he was protected. The two men would keep away from him as long as he was in the company of the constable.

The constable read through Jake's statement, then slid it across the table for Jake to sign. As Jake put his autograph at the bottom, the constable added gravely, 'There may be charges against you in respect of the collisions, sir.'

Jake slid the statement back across the table.

'These are the men responsible,' he said, pointing to his statement.

'You've only given us a description of one man,' the constable pointed out.

'Because I didn't see the other one,' said Jake. 'He was the one holding a gun on me.'

'Yes, sir,' said the constable, not really bothering to hide the note of scepticism in his voice. He read aloud from Jake's statement. 'A short man. About five feet six inches tall. Almost shaven head. Wiry, but with a muscular build. Scar running down the left side of his face from his eye to the corner of his mouth. Dressed in a casual brown zip-up jacket over a black T-shirt. Also wore jeans and trainers.' He looked at Jake.

'Yes.' Jake nodded. 'That was him. The scar makes him very distinctive.' Still playing for time, determined to remain in the safety of the police station for as long as he could, he added, 'If you like, I could go through those book things. The ones with photographs of known criminals, see if I can spot him. I've seen them do that on TV.'

'Yes, well, it's not that easy, sir,' said the constable. 'Everything's computerised these days.'

'I can look at them on a computer,' offered Jake.

The constable stopped short of uttering a heavy sigh. Instead, he said, 'Thank you, sir. I shall contact the ID Department and see if that can be arranged, although it may take a day or two. We'll contact you and make an appointment for you to come in.'

No, you won't, thought Jake. As soon as I've gone, you're just going to file this statement away and hope I forget about it.

The constable stood up.

'Well, sir, if there's nothing more . . .'

No, there isn't, thought Jake ruefully. I have to go out there and hope the pair aren't waiting for me.

'Can I call a taxi from here?' he asked.

'I'm afraid our phones are only for official use,' countered the constable.

'No, I meant, can I call one and wait here for it to arrive?'

The constable studied Jake. He was obviously keen to see the back of him as soon as he could.

'By all means you can wait in the reception area, sir,' he said.

'Thanks,' said Jake.

The constable took him out to the reception area, and he called a cab company he used on an irregular basis. But at least it was one he knew was safe, and he could trust. The cab company assured him they'd pick him up from the police station in fifteen minutes, and he settled himself down in the reception area to wait. He tried phoning Lauren again, both on her landline and her mobile, but each time he got her voicemail. He left the same message both times.

'Lauren, we need to talk. It's urgent. Please ring me.'

As he hung up, he felt worse than ever. Then an awful thought hit him: if the pair of thugs had already been on to him, had others already gone after Lauren? Was that why she wasn't answering her phone?

I have to go round to her flat, he thought. I have to know she's all right. I have to warn her!

A short Asian man came into the station. 'Taxi for Wells?' he said.

'Here,' said Jake, getting up.

He followed the man out and climbed into the taxi, his eyes swivelling as he did so, looking out for any sign of the two men watching him, waiting. He didn't see them, but then, if they were professionals, they'd be sure to be keeping out of sight.

As the taxi made its way through the snarled-up traffic towards north London, Jake tried Lauren's numbers again; but again, there was no answer.

As soon as I get back to my flat, I'll pack a few things in a bag, just in case I have to hide out for a few days, and then go straight to Lauren's and hope she's in.

The taxi pulled up outside his flat. Still nervous, Jake looked around him as he paid the driver, and then hurried to the entrance to the block. No one around, so far.

He used the stairs to get to the first floor, and his flat, rather than risk the lift. At least on the stairs he could see people coming.

There was no one about on his landing. Warily, he checked his front door for any signs that the lock had been forced, but everything seemed normal. Well, as normal as they could be in this nightmare situation.

What's happening? thought Jake desperately. Why is that book so important? And how did those two guys know that it was me who took it?

He unlocked the door of his flat and stepped in, and then stopped. There was something not right, but he couldn't put his finger on it. He hesitated, then shut the front door, just in case anyone was lurking outside on the landing, waiting to follow him inside.

He stood in his small hallway, listening, but there were no sounds other than the usual: the hum of the fridge, the traffic noises outside filtered and muffled by his windows. He sniffed. There was a smell that was

147

different. What was it? Not tobacco. No, a sort of *rusty* smell. Faint, but there.

Apprehensively, he moved towards his kitchen, and suddenly darted past the doorway, glancing in as he did so. His kitchen was empty; he saw that at a glance. It was so tiny there was no room for anyone to hide in it. They wouldn't even have been able to squeeze into any of the kitchen cupboards.

The bathroom was next. The door was shut. Carefully, he pushed the handle down, and then banged the door open, at the same time leaping to one side in case anyone was in there with a gun aimed at the doorway.

There were no shots. No movement or sound at all from the bathroom.

His bedroom was next. The door was half open. Had he left it half open before he went out, or had he closed it? He couldn't remember. He stood outside the room, listening. If anyone was in there, he should be able to hear them breathing. He waited, tense, listening, ears strained. No sound from within the bedroom.

He pushed the bedroom door open and waited, hanging back in the hallway. No gun went off. No one leapt out. Nothing.

I'm getting paranoid, thought Jake. It's just me in the flat. But then he smelt that rusty smell in his nostrils again and thought: but *someone's* been in here since I went out this morning. And maybe they still are.

But where are they? Or maybe the rusty smell was to do with something else: a leaking radiator, maybe. It was quite likely he was being over-sensitive about things, that his imagination was running away with him.

Cautiously, he moved towards his living room. The last room in his flat. If there *was* anyone here, lying in wait for him, this was where they'd be. The living-room door was just slightly ajar. Frantically, he searched his memory: had he closed it like that before he left for work that morning? Or was some-one in there, waiting, poised to pounce as soon as he walked in? He thought he'd left the door open, but he couldn't remember.

He fought to keep down the panic that was rising up inside him.

I shouldn't have come back here, he said to himself. I should have gone to Lauren's first. If she was OK, I should have got her or Parsons to come back here with me. There's less chance of being attacked if I had someone with me.

But right now, he was on his own, vulnerable.

Maybe I should just back out, he thought. I've got this far. Maybe I should retreat to the front door and slip out.

You're overdoing it, he told himself. There's no one here. If there was, they would have been at you by now. They wouldn't have waited this long.

Come on, he urged himself. Open the door and walk

149

in. There's no one there. You're OK. Get in, grab your stuff, and get out.

He hesitated, took a deep breath, then pushed open the door.

There was a body on the floor of his living room. Not just any body, it was the short man who'd stopped him in the street and threatened him. The same black T-shirt, the same short hair, the same scar down one side of his face, only now his eyes were wide open and he was perfectly still, and there was a knife sticking out of his chest.

Jake felt sick. He swayed. Who was this man? How had he got here? Who had killed him? And why?

'I have to phone the police,' he said aloud.

Suddenly, there was a crash from outside his flat, and as he turned he saw the front door being torn off its hinges and hurtling in, and then his flat was filled with men dressed from head to toe in black and holding automatic rifles.

'Face down on the floor!' screamed the man nearest to Jake.

'But . . .' he began.

'On the floor!' roared the man. 'Hands on your head!'

Jake dropped to the floor and pressed his face into the carpet, his hands behind his head, as instructed. All he could see were big boots crashing around him, and then a shout came from one of the men.

150

'Dead, all right! Stabbed!'

Jake started to get up, to explain, but a boot stamped down on the back of his neck, pushing his face back into the carpet.

'Move again and you're dead!'

# Chapter 18

Jake sat in the cell. It was a bare box, with one small window made of wired glass high up in one wall. What was the point of the wired glass? he wondered. The window was about ten feet from the floor, with no way of reaching it, short of being a human fly or Spiderman and climbing up the wall. Maybe it was to stop the prisoners inside the cell from trying to break the glass; but the police sergeant had taken anything hard from Jake: his keys, money. They'd also taken his shoelaces and his tie.

Everything in the cell was fixed down. The metal toilet bowl in one corner. The bench on which he was sitting, and would be sleeping on if they didn't let him out, was a slab of concrete set into the wall. There was a very thin mattress on the concrete slab, but there was no way he could throw the mattress at the window and do any damage to it.

He sat on the mattress on the bench. He'd been here for hours. He didn't know exactly how long because the police had also taken his watch and his mobile. What was it that Albert Einstein had said about time being relative? That sometimes an hour can seem like a day, and sometimes it seems little more than a few seconds. He tried to work out how long he'd been in here. He'd been brought in at about one o'clock. The daylight coming in through the tiny window was still strong, so it was still the afternoon. Why were they leaving him for so long? To soften him up? Frighten him? They'd already done that.

He rubbed the back of his neck. It still ached from where the armed man in black had put his foot on it. He shivered as he remembered the black-clad men with the guns in his flat. Then the plain-clothes people had appeared: a man and a woman. They'd taken one look at Jake, lying on the floor, and at the body of the man in the living room, and then gestured at Jake and said, 'Bring him along.' After that, they'd stripped him of his possessions, and anything they thought he might use to harm himself, and had locked him in this cell.

They think I killed that man, he told himself, and a surge of fear went through him. They'll put me on trial and fix it so I'm found guilty and spend the rest of my life in jail. And all because I saw a man turn into a vegetable! he groaned.

There was the sound of a key in the lock, and then the door swung open. A burly uniformed constable looked in at him.

'All right, you,' he said. 'Someone wants to talk to you.'

'Interview with Jacob Matthew Wells. Detective Inspector Edgar and Sergeant Club attending. PC Omulu also present.'

Jake sat at the bare table, looking across at the man who'd spoken into the recording device, Detective Inspector Edgar. Next to him was Sergeant Club. Jake presumed that the uniformed constable sitting on the rickety chair by the door was PC Omulu.

This room was very different from the interview room in the other police station, where he'd given his statement about being attacked. That room had seemed almost friendly, its walls painted a pastel shade of yellow. This room seemed threatening. The only furniture was the table and a couple of chairs. It smelt musty: stale sweat. The walls were dark. Jake could imagine people being tortured in here with no one coming to help them.

There were no windows, just lights set into the ceiling, their bulbs protected by wire mesh, just like the bulbs in the cell. Jake assumed this was to protect them against people suddenly standing up and throwing

154

a chair at them. He guessed that the table was fixed to the floor. He was tempted to see if it moved and test his theory, but the very grim expression on the face of the detective inspector sitting opposite him told him that would not be a good idea.

'Do you know the dead man?' asked Edgar.

'No,' said Jake.

'But you had seen him before?'

Jake hesitated, then he answered: 'Yes.'

Edgar nodded. He consulted his notes and said, 'You were involved in an incident earlier today at the roundabout by Marsham Street. You gave a statement in which you said you had been the victim of an attempted mugging. Is that right?'

They know, thought Jake.

'Yes,' he said, numbly.

'You described one of the men who attacked you as: about five feet six inches tall, almost shaven head, wearing a black T-shirt with a brown zip-up casual jacket. And with a scar down the left-hand side of his face, from his eyebrow to the corner of his mouth. Is that correct?'

Jake nodded.

'Is the man that was discovered dead in your living room that same man?' asked Edgar.

Jake gulped, then nodded.

'Please answer for the recording,' prompted Edgar.

'Yes,' said Jake.

'Yet you say you don't know this man?'

'That's correct,' said Jake. 'I've never seen him before today. I don't know his name, or anything about him.'

'Yet he was found dead in your flat.'

'That's right.'

The inspector paused, then said, 'Did you invite him into your flat?'

'No,' said Jake. 'I've already told you, he was there when I got home.'

'Alive?'

'No, dead! I've told you that already!'

Edgar remained calm.

'The reason I ask is because there were no signs of a break-in at your flat,' he said. 'Which means either the man was let into the flat by yourself, or someone else.'

'Or he picked the lock,' said Jake.

Edgar looked questioningly at Jake.

'You're suggesting he was burgling your flat?'

'I don't know,' said Jake.

'And someone killed him while he was doing it?'

'Possibly,' said Jake. 'Or he was killed elsewhere and his body dumped in my flat.'

'Why would anyone want to do that?' asked the inspector.

'I don't know,' said Jake again.

The inspector shook his head.

'It's not much of a defence, is it?' he said.

Before Jake could reply, there was a knock at the door, then it opened and a uniformed officer looked in.

'Excuse me, sir,' he said.

He gestured towards the door. The inspector got up and walked over to the uniformed policeman, who whispered something to him. Edgar gave a sigh, and a nod.

'Tell her I'll be out in a moment,' he said.

The uniformed officer nodded, then left, shutting the door behind him.

'Seems like your lawyer's here,' Edgar told Jake.

Jake frowned, puzzled. Lawyer? He didn't have a lawyer.

'Keep an eye on him, Sergeant,' said the inspector. 'I'll be back shortly.' He walked to the desk, said, 'Interview halted at six fifty p.m.' Then he switched off the recorder and walked out of the room.

Jake looked after him, still puzzled. What lawyer?

He stared across the desk at Sergeant Club. Club returned his gaze, his expression impassive. Jake turned towards PC Omulu, on the chair by the door. The constable also looked back at Jake blankly.

No one's giving anything away, thought Jake. They think I killed that man and they want a confession.

They're not going to say anything to me that might give me an excuse in court to claim I was pressurised by them. No friendly smiles, no menacing scowls. Nothing. Just blank expressions.

He turned to studying the dark wall nearest to him. There were bumps and creases in the plaster, and he could make out different shapes. Or, at least, things that looked like shapes. And faces. An eye here, then a nose, and a crack in the plaster that could be a mouth. It was the kind of game he hadn't played since he was a boy at school and the lesson was boring: seeing if he could make faces out of things. A wall. The trunk of a tree. Gravel. He was just starting to see other faces in the dark paint, when the door of the inter-view room opened and Edgar returned. With him was a young woman in a smart suit, carrying a neat black briefcase. Jake guessed her to be in her late twenties. What there was no mistaking, however, was the angry expression on her face. She strode across the room and stopped by Jake.

'Sue Clark from Pierce Randall,' she introduced herself to Jake, her tone clipped and crisp. She looked around the interview room with undisguised disap-proval. 'Do I understand you've been interrogating my client without him having any legal representation?' she snapped at Edgar.

Inspector Edgar bridled.

'I hardly think "interrogating" is the right word . . .'
he began.

'Oh. And what is the right word, might I ask?'
demanded Clark. Her voice cut through the air like a
whip. 'It looks to me as if there have been so many
infringements in my client's rights that you'll be lucky
if you stay in your job.'

She's tough, thought Jake. She's the one I want on
my side. But how did I get her?

'Now look here . . .' protested Edgar.

'No, you look,' interrupted Clark firmly. 'As I understand it, my client is just a witness, yet it's obvious
he's being treated as a suspect. This is not due process.
Now, if you don't want to find yourself a subject of a
major investigation, I suggest you release my client.'

'At the moment he's helping us with our enquiries,'
countered Edgar.

'And he will return and continue to help you with
those enquiries after he and I have had our discussion
about this case,' stated Clark. 'Don't forget, Inspector,
we are Pierce Randall. You may have heard of us.'

It was pretty obvious from the unhappy expression on
the detective's face that he had, and it wasn't good news.

'Very well,' he growled. 'In the spirit of cooperation,
we shall release Mr Wells.' Then he added quickly, 'But
be aware that his home is now a crime scene, and we
cannot have that tampered with.'

159

'That's no problem,' said Clark. 'Pierce Randall have an apartment Mr Wells can move into for the time being. This is the address.' She produced a card which she handed to Edgar. 'But, if you wish to make contact with Mr Wells for any reason before we return, you will do that through me. My contact details are on the reverse side of the card.'

'Very well.' Edgar nodded. 'We would like Mr Wells to return to help us with our enquiries tomorrow morning at nine thirty.' His tone changed to one of pointed sarcasm as he asked, 'Will that be all right with you?'

Clark nodded. 'That is acceptable. We will report here at nine thirty a.m. tomorrow.' Turning to Jake, she said, 'Do you have any possessions here?'

'My mobile and my keys,' said Jake, his mind still in a whirl at the effect this woman had had on his situation. 'And my shoelaces.'

'Let's collect them and then we can go,' she said.

Jake got to his feet and followed the lawyer to the door. A uniformed officer opened it for them.

I'm out! thought Jake. Free!

But then the additional disturbing thought returned: who is she? And what is she leading me into?

# Chapter 19

There was a car waiting for them in the parking area outside the police station. Not just any car: this was a luxurious-looking Merc with blacked-out windows, the number plates showing it was this year's model, and standing beside it was a uniformed chauffeur who opened the rear door for them.

Jake got in and sank into the plush leather seating. My God, he thought. I've been in hotel rooms that weren't as comfortable as this!

The chauffeur slid behind the steering wheel and the car moved off. Jake noticed there was a glass panel between the driver and the rear of the car.

'Who are you?' he asked.

Clark frowned. 'I thought I'd introduced myself,' she said.

'Yes, but *who* are you? I mean, where did you come from? Who sent you?'

'I'll let my principal deal with your questions,' she said. 'He's better equipped for that. My job was just to get you out of there, and then represent you in any further interviews you may have with the police.'

'Like tomorrow morning,' said Jake.

She shrugged. 'A formality,' she said. 'I'm pretty confident they won't be troubling you after that.'

Jake regarded her, baffled at her confidence.

'How can you say that?' he asked. 'They found a dead man in my flat, and no sign of a break-in.'

'We are Pierce Randall,' she said simply.

Jake shook his head.

'I've never heard of you,' he said.

'Very few people have,' said Clark. 'The important thing is that the ones who matter have heard of us. Now, if you'll excuse me, I need to check my messages, and send a few myself.'

'About me?'

Clark almost smiled.

'You're not our only client, Mr Wells. At any one moment we are juggling many cases.' She pointed at some magazines in a compartment in the door next to him. 'You'll find some reading material there, if you get bored.'

But he didn't feel like reading anything at the moment. He was still getting used to being trapped as a suspected murderer one moment, and then riding to freedom in this luxury car the next.

The car was silent and smooth; he hardly noticed it was moving. He sat and watched the world go by, while beside him Sue Clark's fingers were busy with her state-of-the art mobile, reading and replying to messages. Where are we going? he wondered. From the street signs it looked as if they were heading south-east, towards Docklands. Sure enough, soon he saw the new high-rise luxury apartment blocks of Docklands ahead. The new City money. The Merc turned through some side streets, and then pulled up in front of an enormous pair of steel gates. The driver pressed something on the dashboard, and the gates slowly rumbled open. The driver let the car roll through and down a slope. The gates moved slowly shut again after them.

'Secure parking,' explained Clark, putting her mobile phone away. 'It goes with the apartment.'

'Whose apartment?' asked Jake.

'Yours, for the moment,' said Clark. 'Remember what the detective said: your own flat is a crime scene. So you'll be staying here for the moment, until we can get that changed. It should only be for a short while. Hopefully, we'll be able to get it sorted at tomorrow morning's meeting.'

The car pulled up into a parking bay. Clark got out.

'Wait here,' she instructed the chauffeur. 'We'll be back shortly.'

She set off for the lifts. Jake hurried after her.

'Are we in a hurry?' he asked, impressed by the fast pace at which she walked.

'Life is a hurry,' she said. 'Every minute that passes we're one minute nearer to dying. Life is too short to waste it by dawdling.'

She pressed the call button, and the lift doors opened. Again, Jake was met with luxury: the voice-activation which asked for the required floor level; the carpets, the décor. As with the car, Jake reflected he'd lived in worse places than this lift.

They got out of the lift at the twenty-third floor. Once again, Clark set off at a fast pace along a quiet corridor, then stopped at the door of an apartment and keyed in a security code beside it.

'I'll give you the codes later,' she said. 'It's a lot more secure than keys.'

Inside, the apartment was everything that Jake expected, after the Merc and the lift: luxury and money, but in a minimalist style. In the living room were tables and chairs made of steel, chrome and glass. The cupboards were hidden in the walls, painted black. The walls were also black, but with large paintings and mirrors hanging to give the apartment colour.

'Bedroom through there,' said Clark, pointing.

'Bathroom. Separate wet room. Kitchen. It's simple, but it serves.'

Simple, thought Jake. If she thinks this is simple, what would she make of my flat?

'You'll be perfectly safe here,' Clark told Jake. 'Later, we'll get some things sorted out ahead of tomorrow morning, but right now I suggest you get yourself freshened up; then my principal wishes to see you. I'll just let him know we're back.'

She was walking towards the landline phone on the table, when her mobile rang.

'Sue Clark,' she said briskly. Then her tone changed: 'Mr Munro. I was just about to call you. I have Mr Wells with me . . .'

The caller didn't allow her to finish. He had obviously told her to switch on the TV, because she picked up a remote control, clicked it, and a TV news channel appeared on the screen. There was a picture of Carl Parsons on the screen.

'I've got it,' she said.

She increased the volume, and Jake heard the newsreader say: 'The body has been identified as that of Carl Parsons, a student.' As Jake watched, his mouth open in shock, the picture of Parsons was replaced by one of Lauren. 'Police are looking for a woman, Lauren Graham, also a student. They have urged the public not to confront this woman, but to contact the police

165

immediately if they see her. Full details have not yet been disclosed, but we will be giving an update as soon as we know more. In other news . . .'

Clark switched to mute, and the sound vanished, leaving the newsreader mouthing silently. Jake stared at the screen, still stunned by what he just had seen and heard. Parsons dead! The police looking for Lauren! It couldn't be true! Clark was talking into her mobile.

'Yes, Mr Munro. I'll send Mr Wells to your office right away.' She hung up and turned to Jake. 'This is a bad turn of events.'

'Someone's killed Carl Parsons!' blurted out Jake, shocked.

'And they think Ms Graham did it.' Clark nodded sombrely.

'Impossible!' said Jake. 'Lauren wouldn't hurt anyone! Least of all Carl!'

Clark moved to her laptop and began to search for postings of the story on the web.

'Let's see what there is,' she murmured. On her screen appeared the photos of Lauren and Parsons. She read swiftly through the accompanying text. 'His body was found in his flat three hours ago,' she said. 'He'd been dead for about an hour.' She allowed herself a small smile. 'At least you're off the hook for *his* murder. Being in a police cell is the best alibi there is.'

Jake hurried over to join her and read the text over her shoulder as she scrolled down. Parsons had been stabbed. There were signs of a struggle. The police had received 999 calls reporting a disturbance from the flat: shouts and screams. Almost immediately afterwards, Lauren had been seen hurrying away from the block of flats by two separate witnesses. Later, the police arrived and broke into the flat, and found Parsons's body.

'Strong evidence against her,' muttered Clark.

'Nonsense!' stormed Jake. 'It wasn't her! It was someone who looked like her!'

Clark went to another website where the story was featured. This one had an image of Lauren coming out of the block of flats, with the time in white lettering underneath.

'CCTV footage,' said Clark. 'Someone's worked fast.'

'It's faked,' said Jake, shaking his head. 'It has to be!'

'Or she did it,' said Clark. She pointed at the image of Lauren on the screen. 'He's killed in his flat, and minutes later she's running away from it.'

'Maybe that's what it is,' said Jake. 'She's running away! From whoever killed Parsons!'

'So why didn't she phone nine-nine-nine?'

Jake hesitated, then shrugged. 'I don't know,' he said. 'Maybe she lost her mobile.'

'There's a public phone box not far away, according to this report,' said Clark, continuing to read. 'That's where one of the calls about the disturbance at the flat came from.'

'Maybe she was in a panic,' said Jake. 'Someone was chasing her!'

Clark shook her head. 'There's nothing about anyone else seen leaving the flats at the same time. Just Ms Graham.' She turned to Jake and gave him a look of sympathy. 'You have to admit to the possibility that she did it.'

'No!' Jake told her firmly. 'Why would she?'

'Maybe he attacked her,' suggested Clark. 'She defended herself, there was a struggle, he got stabbed. She panics and runs.'

A thought suddenly hit Jake.

'What was he stabbed with?' he asked.

Clark scrolled down and they both read the text.

'According to this . . .' began Clark.

'A kitchen knife!' said Jake triumphantly. 'The same thing the dead man in my flat was stabbed with!'

Clark looked back at him, questioningly.

'Don't you see!' implored Jake. 'It's the same MO, or whatever the police call it. Use a kitchen knife that's already there so it's got fingerprints already on it. In my case, my fingerprints. In this case, Lauren's. She likes cooking. She'd have used the knife to chop vegetables, or whatever.' He stabbed his finger at the laptop screen. 'I bet you the same person who killed Carl Parsons killed the man in my flat!'

'It's possible,' she said. 'Which means it's possible that person was your Lauren Graham.'

Jake stared back at her.

'That's ridiculous!' he said.

'Is it?' she asked. 'What do you know about her?'

'I went out with her for a long time!'

'What do you call a long time?'

'Six months.'

'And you haven't seen her for how long?'

'Until the other day, about two months.'

Clark sighed.

'Mr Wells, we don't always know people as well as we think we do. There are millions of cases of bigamists, where the husband or wife didn't know their partner had another family; people who apparently are respectable people who are actually criminals or killers or spies . . .'

'Lauren is none of those,' said Jake firmly. 'For a start, she wouldn't have even been involved in this if I hadn't brought her into it. *I* phoned *her*!'

Clark looked as if she was about to say something, then she obviously changed her mind. Instead, she shrugged.

'Very well,' she said. 'But all I ask is you consider it as an option. Keep an open mind.'

'No,' replied Jake firmly, shaking his head.

Clark shrugged again.

'OK,' she said. 'Anyway, right now Mr Munro wants to see you.'

'Mr Munro?'

'He's the man who hired me to get you out of jail.'

# Chapter 20

They returned to the Merc in the underground car park. This time, Clark didn't get in. 'You and Mr Munro won't need me for this meeting,' she said. She indicated the uniformed chauffeur, standing with the rear door of the car open. 'Keith will take you to Mr Munro and bring you back afterwards. I'll call and pick you up at eight forty-five tomorrow morning.'

'Don't we need to discuss what we're going to say tomorrow?' asked Jake.

'You won't say anything,' said Clark. 'I'll do the talking.' She handed him a plastic card. On it were printed sequences of numbers. 'The code at the top is the key to get into the apartment. The one at the bottom is to get into the building.' She shrugged. 'Not that you'll need that one. Once Keith brings you back, I think you'll be ready to go to bed. My advice would be to get a good night's sleep so we're ready for the police tomorrow.' She turned to the chauffeur. 'Take him to Mr Munro's,' she said. 'And bring him back safely.'

'Yes, Ms Clark.' Keith nodded.

There was something about Keith, the way he held himself, his build, that suggested to Jake he was more than just a chauffeur. A bodyguard, thought Jake. Former SAS, I bet. Just like those two men who grabbed me in Marsham Street.

Clark headed towards another car in a nearby parking bay, this one a low-slung silver sports car. How the other half live, thought Jake. Luxury apartments. Mercs. Silver sports cars. They never have to worry about battling to get on to a crowded tube train, or be concerned about increases in their electricity bills. Nothing but the best for them. Expense no object. Even when one of them is arrested for murder, they have the clout to walk them out of police custody and away to somewhere safe. Money and power.

Once again, Jake settled into the luxury of the leather seats in the rear of the Merc, and let Keith do the work. His thoughts were full of Lauren and Parsons. What had happened? It had to be the same sort of thugs who'd been after him, only they'd caught up with Lauren and Parsons, and Parsons had been killed and Lauren framed for his murder. But who was behind it?

Jake glanced at the back of Keith's head through the glass partition. Yes, definitely a military man. Ex-special forces, he was sure. Just like the dead man in his flat. Jake felt a sudden jolt of fear at the thought of being driven by this military man to see the mysterious Mr Munro. Was this Munro the person behind all that had happened? He certainly had the sort of power to make things happen, if the apartment and what had happened with Detective Inspector Edgar was anything to go by. Was he being taken unsuspectingly into some kind of spider's lair?

You've seen too many James Bond films, Jake warned himself. Too many films where the villain is some super-rich man, pulling the strings, above any law. He wondered what this Munro character would be like. A James Bond super-villain? Sitting in a magnificent luxury apartment, like the one they'd just left? Maybe stroking a white cat with a jewelled necklace round its neck?

For heaven's sake, stop letting your imagination run away with you, Jake told himself. This is real life, not some thriller! But someone *had* tried to kill him. Someone had killed Carl Parsons. Someone had killed the dead man in Jake's flat.

He noticed the car slowing down, and realised they'd pulled into yet another underground car park. The car stopped, and Keith got out and opened the rear door for him.

'Number three lift, sir,' he said, gesturing to a row of lift doors. 'It will take you straight to the company's offices.'

'Which company is that?' asked Jake.

Keith seemed surprised by the question.

'Pierce Randall, of course, sir,' he said.

'Of course.' Jake nodded.

'I'll be waiting for you when you've finished,' said Keith.

Jake nodded, and went to the lift. As he approached the doors, they opened. Automatic sensors, registered Jake. More luxury. He stepped in, and the doors closed, and the lift shot up at speed. If Munro is a real villain, I'm trapped, thought Jake. There's no way out. Keith is guarding the only way out, and he could kill me with one hand.

The lift doors slid open and Jake stepped warily out. It was no James Bond villain who was waiting to greet him: no one with black-gloved metal claws for hands; or a golden gun; and certainly not a malicious-looking white cat. The man who greeted Jake was medium height, about forty, dressed in a plain but expensive-looking suit, and with a warm friendly smile on his face. It was the first warm and friendly smile Jake had seen in some time. Except for Gareth's; but Jake already knew that Gareth's smile was a complete fake.

174

'Mr Wells.' The man beamed. 'I'm Alex Munro, a senior partner with the London office of Pierce Randall. It's a pleasure to finally meet you.'

Jake let his hand be shaken in welcome. It was a good handshake: firm and friendly, just like Munro's smile.

'I'm sure you're bursting with questions,' said Munro. 'So why don't we go into my office and get acquainted, and I can answer everything.'

They walked along a corridor decorated with heavy carpet. On either side were large offices, with people in shirtsleeves at their desks, on the phone, or sitting intently at computer screens. Jake looked at his watch. It was 8 p.m.

'You've got a lot of people working late,' he commented.

Munro smiled. 'There is no such concept as "working late" at Pierce Randall,' he said. 'We are a global firm. Some of them are talking to clients in Australia, where it is early in the morning. The fact is, we operate twenty-four hours a day, because the world operates twenty-four hours a day.' He came to an office door and pushed it open for Jake to enter.

It was a large office, but hardly luxurious. Certainly not when compared to Gareth's, for example. The chairs were simple and minimalist, but looked comfortable. The large desk had a few files on it, a few sheets of paper, but not much else. Neither cluttered, nor clear.

'Please, take a seat, Mr Wells,' said Munro, gesturing at a chair. 'Or may I call you Jake?'

'Please do.' Jake nodded.

Munro's smile broadened.

'In that case, please call me Alex,' he said. 'It's far less formal. We like to think of our clients as our friends at Pierce Randall.'

Jake sat down.

'Anything to drink?' asked Munro. 'Tea? Coffee? Brandy? Beer?'

'No thanks,' replied Jake.

The truth was, he'd love to sink a beer right now, but he was feeling so shattered he was worried if he did he'd do or say something stupid, and he felt he needed to be on his guard, however friendly Alex Munro seemed to be.

Munro settled himself down in an equally comfortable chair opposite Jake, and nodded sympathetically.

'Getting right to the point, we know you were framed,' he said, his face serious. 'That dead man in your flat.'

'I'm not the only one!' burst out Jake. 'This business of Lauren and Carl . . .'

'Ah, Ms Graham.' Munro nodded thoughtfully. 'We'll get to her in a moment.'

'What happened to her and Parsons is connected with the book,' insisted Jake.

'Absolutely,' agreed Munro. 'I have no doubt of that whatsoever.'

'She's innocent!'

Munro hesitated, then nodded.

'I know you think so, and you may well be right . . .'

'I *am* right!' said Jake emphatically. He calmed himself down, then said apologetically, 'I'm sorry for flying off the handle. This has all been such a nightmare! It's been unbelievable! Sue Clark told me you hired her to represent me.' He looked at Munro, puzzled. 'I'm still not sure how you even knew I was in custody.'

'There are lots of things you don't know, Jake. Maybe I'd better explain. It all begins with the secret library of the Order of Malichea.'

Jake studied him, his mind whirling.

'You mean you believe in the secret library?' he asked carefully.

Munro nodded. 'Absolutely,' he said. 'And that the monks hid the books in the fifteenth century.'

Jake regarded him, still puzzled.

'I don't understand why you're involved,' he said. 'Why are you interested in these ancient books? It hardly fits with a powerful, modern, twenty-first century law firm.'

Munro smiled. 'I'm afraid our image belies what lies at the heart of Pierce Randall. The firm was set up early in the twentieth century by two idealist solicitors in Edinburgh, and they set it up for one reason only: to get justice and fair play for all. I admit, that since those days, the firm has gone on to occupy a very grand sphere in the legal world, but the basic principal remains the same: justice and fair play for all.

'In the case of the hidden science texts, we believe that the information they contain could be invaluable to the whole of humanity. They could hold the answers to disease, famine . . .'

'That's what Lauren said,' said Jake unhappily. He sighed. 'I'm guessing that with all the hoo-ha that's going on, the book that was dug up at the site is the first one ever found.'

Munro shook his head.

'No,' he said. 'I know of at least one that's been discovered, and I believe there have been others that have been found, but kept hidden.'

'Who by?' asked Jake.

'I would suggest your own people,' said Munro.

'My own people?' asked Jake, puzzled.

'The Department of Science. That's what they did with this book, isn't it? The one that was dug up at the site.'

Jake hesitated. That was exactly what had happened. And if they'd done that with *this* particular book . . .

Suddenly the implication of what Munro had just said struck Jake. *I know of at least one*. '*You've* got one,' he challenged.

Munro nodded. 'We found one for one of our clients. Nothing startling. Not like the text that I understand you saw dug up, Jake. The one we found is about the science of optics. Basically, creating spectacles to help those with poor vision.' He smiled. 'But the miraculous aspect of it is that it was written in 200 BC. Yours was on the rapid growth of fungal spores, I believe.'

'That's what Lauren said,' replied Jake. 'By some guy called . . .' he struggled to recall the name. 'El Izmir something . . .'

'El Izmir Al Tabul. The greening of the desert,' said Munro. 'Creating food from fungal spores.' He nodded thoughtfully. 'It's on our list.'

Jake studied Munro suspiciously.

'You've got a list?'

'Yes,' said Munro. 'One we've compiled over many years, based on rumours of what the secret library contained.'

'Lauren's got a list like that,' said Jake.

'We'd like to take a look at it,' said Munro. 'Compare the two lists.'

'Let's find her first,' said Jake grimly.

'We're working on that already,' said Munro calmly. 'As you've already pointed out, we are a very large and very rich organisation. As a law firm, one of our briefs is to trace people. The private investigators we employ are second to none. If anyone can find Ms Graham, they can.'

'They need to do it before whoever killed Carl gets to her.'

Munro hesitated. He's about to tell me that Lauren killed Carl, thought Jake. Then Munro obviously changed his mind.

'Let's worry about that later,' he said. 'Can we return to why we had you freed?'

'The book,' said Jake.

'The book.' Munro nodded. 'The El Izmir. The one you and Ms Graham rescued from Hadley Park last night.'

He knows, Jake said to himself. He's not just guessing. In the same way that Gareth knew, and those two men who grabbed me in the street. And Penny Johnson. Everyone involved in this case knows that Lauren and I got the book. How? Was it the image of Lauren and him on the CCTV, even though he had been masked? Then another thought struck him.

'This book you found for your clients – the one about optics . . .'

'Yes,' said Munro.

'There's nothing about it having been found on the internet. If there had been, Lauren would have known. She's been trying to trace this hidden library for years, even to find one book from it just so she can prove it exists.'

'A very worthy ambition,' said Munro.

'So why haven't you announced this book you found to the world? If what you say is true, about wanting to share the knowledge with everyone.'

'We thought about that,' said Munro. 'But then we reasoned, if we did and word got out that it was one of the Malichea hidden books, every crackpot would be out searching and digging. And who knows where these books might end up? In the hands of crooks, or governments who want to keep them hidden.'

'But you're keeping this one hidden,' persisted Jake.

'Believe me, Jake, if it had anything new to show the world, we would reveal it. We would give that information to the world, freely. But, unlike the text you found, all our book says about optical sciences is already known.'

Jake studied Munro. Despite the man's easy manner, the frank way he spoke about everything and the way he'd answered all of his questions, Jake had an uneasy feeling there was something being hidden.

'You were talking about the book,' Jake reminded him.

'The one you have,' said Munro, watching him intently.

Jake shook his head.

'I haven't got it. You're right, Lauren and I took it last night, but she and Carl Parsons took it with them. The idea was for Parsons to take care of it because he was less likely to have his flat burgled. Also, he said he could hide it better than either of us.'

'Do you know where?' asked Munro.

'No,' admitted Jake.

'A pity,' sighed Munro.

'Find Lauren,' said Jake. 'She'll know where it is. She may even have it with her.'

Munro nodded.

'I still don't get it,' said Jake. He waved his hand around at the luxurious offices. 'All this costs money to keep up. Someone's got to pay for it. Likewise, searching the world for the hidden texts must cost a huge amount.' He gave Munro a quizzical look. 'No matter how much you may care for the "common good", there's got to be a reason why you pour so much money into searching for these books. You've got to get paid for it.'

A small smile crossed Munro's face. 'Money, indeed, Jake. The force that seems to drive the world. But, in this case, not necessarily so. As you rightly point out, the search for the books does cost a great deal of money. But fortunately we are the kind of firm with many very wealthy clients, and not all of them want to keep the money for themselves. I'm sure you know about Bill Gates and Microsoft pumping millions into Third World health charities?'

'You're saying he's one of your clients?'

'No,' said Munro. 'I'm just giving you that as an example. We have many wealthy clients who feel that the hidden texts should be found, and the information and discoveries used to make this world a better place. They channel their money to us to try to make that a reality.' He sighed. 'Unfortunately, of course, we are up against very powerful oppositions.'

'The government,' said Jake bitterly, thinking about Gareth and the Department of Science.

'Not just the government of this country,' said Munro. 'Other governments, especially those who fear these discoveries could result in dangerous new weapons. And large chemical companies who make millions from selling drugs, just because they hold the patents on them. There are many organisations who want to make sure that these books are never found.

'There are other companies who want the books so they can patent the sciences in them, and so make massive profits from them. There are also weapons manufacturers and terrorist organisations who would love to get hold of some of the sciences and use them as weapons. Like this El Izmir book on fungal spores, for example. Look what happened to that worker who was contaminated at the site by the spores. Imagine that on a massive scale. A biological weapon that doesn't destroy buildings. That's a potential gold mine!' His tone suddenly became very serious. 'It also represents a threat of nightmare proportions. That's why it's vital that book doesn't fall into the wrong hands.'

Jake nodded. 'Yes, I see,' he said. 'But I don't know where I fit in.'

'Because you have seen the book. You know it exists. And because Ms Graham obviously trusts you. If she *is* out there and she's going to get in touch with anyone, I believe that will be you.' He leant forward, the expression on his face now deadly concerned. 'You are the key to finding this book. We got you out of jail because we need you to help us find it. For the good of the world.' His face softened. 'It's also what Ms Graham wants.'

'Yes,' admitted Jake. It was. Bring the hidden library out into the open, for the common good.

Munro sat back, relaxed.

'So, can we count on your help?' he asked.

'Right now the book isn't as important as finding Lauren,' Jake responded. 'But if finding the book will help find Lauren and get her back safely, and it seems that's the case, then yes, you can count on my help.'

'Excellent!' Munro beamed. He looked at his watch. 'It's getting late. You must be tired.'

Yes, I am, realised Jake. I've been running on adrenalin ever since those two men tried to kill me in Marsham Street, and now it's wearing off. I need to sleep.

'The car will take you back to the apartment,' said Munro. 'Get yourself a good night's sleep, and remember you have an appointment with Ms Clark and the police tomorrow morning.'

'I won't forget,' said Jake.

'Good,' said Munro. 'Oh, and if you need anything at all during the night, or if you feel alarmed, there is a concierge on duty twenty-four hours a day. Just pick up the red handset.'

'All-round protection,' commented Jake.

'Nothing is too good for our clients,' said Munro.

# Chapter 21

Keith dropped Jake off in the underground car park, and Jake went through the security systems for the lift and the door to the apartment, still half expecting someone to leap out and attack him the whole time. Even when he got into the apartment, he went from room to room, checking to make sure no one was hiding anywhere in it.

I'm not paranoid, he told himself, just terrified.

He went into the kitchen and stood studying the equipment. Everything looked very hi-tech, as if it all needed a degree in computing to operate. I need a coffee, he said to himself. Luckily, the kettle seemed simple enough. He was just filling it with water when his mobile rang. Lauren, he thought as he snatched it up and pressed connect.

'Lauren?'

'No, sorry,' said a woman's voice. It was Penny Johnson, the reporter.

'I don't need this,' said Jake wearily. 'I've had a very very bad day.'

'I know,' said Johnson.

'No, you don't,' said Jake.

'Last night you took a book from Hadley Park Research Establishment. A man was found dead in your flat. You were arrested as a suspect. You've got to go back for questioning tomorrow morning. Your ex-girlfriend is on the run, accused of killing her boyfriend. You've just got in from seeing Alex Munro of Pierce Randall. How am I doing?'

Jake hesitated. This didn't sound like some reporter on a local newspaper; unless she was gathering credits to get a job on one of the majors.

'We need to talk,' said Johnson.

'I don't think I want to talk to you.'

'It could help Lauren,' said Johnson.

Jake was silent for a moment. It was a con, he was sure of it. She was just a journalist looking for a story. But he remembered their previous meeting, when she'd dropped that she knew about the Order of Malichea, and her closing words: *The book needs to go back to its rightful owners*. Penny Johnson was involved in this case, and not just as a reporter.

'OK,' he said. 'Come and see me. I'm at –'

'I know where you are,' she interrupted him. 'It's too dangerous for me. There's a bar at the corner of the street, The Lounge. I'll see you there in five minutes.'

The phone went dead.

*Too dangerous for me?* Jake thought. Where was the danger? This apartment had to be one of the safest places on the planet. If he left here, he'd be out in the open, definitely at risk. But she'd used the magic words: *It could help Lauren.*

The Lounge sounded like the kind of bar you'd expect to find in some swish upmarket hotel. It wasn't. Away from the plush expensiveness of the apartment block, the street became a series of boarded-up terraced houses awaiting development. Jake guessed they would become part of the new upmarket Pierce Randall development, more hi-tech apartments. Old London disappearing to make way for New London. Just past the boarded-up houses was The Lounge, a dingy-looking pub on the corner. The sound of thumping early sixties music came from it. It's going to be full of geezers, thought Jake apprehensively. Geezers and old-time gangsters. He felt nervous just pushing open the door.

To his surprise, the pub was nearly empty. Just a few people, mainly men, sitting at tables with pints of ale in front of them. This clientele was a far cry from the high-flying financial whizz-kids of the city, and the lawyers from Pierce Randall in their expensive suits.

The men in here were mainly middle-aged or old, and wearing suits that had gone out of fashion decades ago. If they were ever in fashion. No one looked like a hard man, or a special forces soldier.

The clientele looked at Jake as he came in, and then disregarded him, turning back to their talk of football, betting, the telly, and how much better things used to be in the old days.

They'll be gone soon, reflected Jake. Like the buildings. Once the new hi-tech buildings are here, this pub will be gone, or turned into a yuppie watering hole, filled with the sounds of Blackberries and iPhones going off, and these old guys will have to find somewhere else to go.

He looked around the pub and saw Penny Johnson sitting alone at a corner table with a glass in front of her. No one was near her. Jake walked over to the table and sat down.

'What's all this stuff about the apartment being too dangerous?' he asked. 'That place is a lot safer than here.'

'The whole apartment block is owned by Pierce Randall.'

'So?'

She gestured towards the back of the pub.

'See the door to the toilets?'

Jake nodded.

'Yes,' he said.

'It leads to a back door out on to the street. A fire exit. Go out and wait for me. I'll join you in a minute.'

'Why?' asked Jake.

'Because at least two people have already been killed so far,' said Johnson. 'I don't intend to be the next victim.'

As Jake walked towards the fire exit he thought to himself, Why am I doing this? Why am I following her instructions? People have tried to kill me. For all I know, she's got a couple of heavies waiting for me as soon as I step into the street.

He hesitated, then stopped and turned. Johnson was sitting at the table, sipping at her drink, as if everything was normal. She saw him looking back at her, and winked and smiled.

What's that about? thought Jake. A wink and a smile, at a time like this! Then it hit him; she was playing a role, just in case anyone was watching. He looked around. There didn't seem to be any suspicious characters in here. Well, not many. But then again, what did a suspicious character look like? Not all of them had knife scars down one side of their face. There was something suspicious about Sue Clark, for example. But then, she was a lawyer.

He looked again at Johnson, and this time she raised an eyebrow questioningly at him.

I should walk back and tell her I'm not going outside that door, he thought. If she's got anything to tell me, she can tell me here and now.

Then he thought: but she seems to know what's going on. And if she doesn't want to talk here, there has to be a reason for it. And she did say that what she has to say could help Lauren.

He turned back towards the door leading to the toilets and the fire exit.

The alley at the back of the pub was dark. There was one street light some distance away, with a bulb that flickered, casting an eerie on-off light on the back door, throwing many shadows. In any one of those shadows someone could be waiting, with a gun aimed at him, or a knife ready to stick into him.

He shivered at the thought, and at the cold wind that chilled him. It was late and it was dark and it was cold. Where was Penny Johnson? He looked at the back door, waiting for her to appear. Hurry up, he urged her silently, feeling very vulnerable.

Suddenly, he heard the sound of boots approaching. He spun round. The alley was empty. The boots were approaching from a side road.

It was a trap! he thought. She sold me out!

He hurried to the back door of the pub, but found it jammed shut. It was a fire exit that only opened outwards. There was no way back into the pub that way.

He broke into a run, heading away from the pub, towards the flickering street light. At least it would offer some form of sanctuary; they might not attack him by a light, where their faces might be caught and identified on CCTV. As he reached the corner of the building, a figure clad in leathers and wearing a motor-cycle helmet stepped out and crashed into him.

'I haven't got it!' he yelled defensively, throwing up his hands to defend himself against the blows he expected to rain down on him.

'I know you haven't, you idiot!' snapped a young woman's voice. Johnson!

Jake gaped at her face looking back at him in annoyance.

'What was all that business of hanging about in the pub?' she demanded.

'I didn't know if I could trust you,' he said. 'And, anyway, what took you so long?'

She gestured at her motorbike leathers. 'These don't slip on in just seconds,' she said. She held out her hand, and Jake realised she was holding a second motorcycle helmet. 'Here,' she said. 'Put this on.'

'Why?' asked Jake.

'Because it's against the law to ride a motorbike without one,' she said. 'Even pillion.'

# Chapter 22

The journey on Penny Johnson's motorbike was one of the scariest rides of Jake's life. He'd hoped that she would have something small and discreet, but when she strode over to what looked like something out of a Hell's Angel movie, his heart sank. She climbed on and kick-started it into life, then gestured for Jake to sit behind her. No sooner was he sat down, than the bike roared off, the acceleration almost pulling him off backwards. Jake had been determined to try to be cool and macho and keep his hands casually behind him. That determination soon vanished, and he wrapped his arms around Johnson's front. This meant that, even though it was August, his hands were soon freezing from the cold wind, but he hung on grimly as the bike zoomed and swerved in and out of the London traffic.

It seemed like an eternity before Johnson pulled the bike to a halt and switched off the engine.

'Here,' she said. 'Bring the helmet.'

Jake undid his helmet and followed Johnson as she headed towards a cybercafé. She was obviously well-known there, because the guy at the desk just waved at her in a friendly manner and she went to an empty screen and sat down. Jake pulled up a spare chair and sat down beside her.

'Why here?' he demanded. 'We could have used any computer. They've got one at the apartment.'

'This one isn't bugged,' she told him.

Jake shivered. He still felt frozen from the bike ride.

'What's going on?' he asked.

'I'm going to show you a little about Pierce Randall,' she said. 'Your lawyers.'

Her fingers had stopped dancing over the keyboard, and now a web page appeared with the logo that Jake had seen when he'd stepped out of the lift and met Alex Munro. Pierce Randall's website.

'I could have seen all this at the firm itself,' Jake complained.

'True,' said Johnson. 'But I want you to see both sides.'

She moved her chair so Jake could get nearer and have a clearer view of the screen.

'Wow!' he said as he scrolled down their client list. He could see why the police had been keen to cooperate with Sue Clark and let him go. Well, all right, not exactly 'keen', but Inspector Edgar hadn't been prepared to stand up to her. It was as Clark had said to him: he may not have heard of Pierce Randall, but plenty of others had. And very influential people at that.

'No wonder the police backed off,' he murmured. 'That's a pretty impressive list of clients. Multinational companies and banks, some very, *very* important people, and some pretty powerful governments. This is a company with major clout.'

'In more ways than one,' said Johnson. She ran her fingers over the keyboard again, and the website vanished, to be replaced by a message board headed 'PR Watch'. This contained different postings, but all mentioning Pierce Randall as being in some way connected to very different people and organisations than those Pierce Randall proudly trumpeted on their website. Jake recognised some of the names: vicious tyrannical dictators who ruled countries in Africa and the Far East. Reputed gangsters and arms dealers. Other familiar names popped up: corrupt politicians, suspected terrorists, billionaires with dubious reputations; the Mafia, both Sicilian and Russian.

'An interesting client list, don't you think?' asked Johnson.

Jake shook his head as he gestured at the screen.

'It's all rumour and innuendo,' he said. 'As a journalist you must know none of this carries any real weight. These postings are just by people with axes to grind against the firm, making accusations. Some of them pretty wild, as well.'

'Some of them are true,' said Johnson seriously.

'OK.' Jake shrugged. 'So maybe they do also represent some dodgy people. That's what being a lawyer is all about. Not every client is innocent.'

Johnson pointed at the screen.

'Some of those are more than just "not innocent",' she pointed out. 'They're killers and terrorists and gangsters . . .'

'Alleged,' countered Jake. 'If they really were as guilty as everyone here says, why aren't they in jail?'

Johnson gave a wry smile.

'Because the gangsters and dictators make up the laws in their own countries,' she said. 'And the others, well, they have a firm of very good lawyers representing them.'

Jake hesitated, then nodded. He remembered how Clark had got him out of that terrifying interview room.

'OK,' he admitted. 'Maybe they do represent some dodgy people. But so what? And how does this fit in with what happened at Hadley Park, and Lauren? And where do you fit in? And don't tell me it's because you're a journalist on a story.'

'I'll tell you,' she said. 'Come on.'

She got up and headed for the door, and Jake felt a chill of fear going through him.

'We're going on the bike again?' he asked apprehensively.

'No,' said Johnson. 'There's a place next door we can talk without being overheard, even if we're bugged.'

The place next door was a bar, but not just an ordinary bar. It was a bikers' bar. Everybody in it, with the exception of Jake, seemed to be dressed in motorbike leathers; mostly black, but some multicoloured, and one even in pink. The music was loud: a mixture of heavy metal and garage.

It was Johnson who pushed her way to the bar, squeezing between the crush of bikers, and returned with two glasses of a clear liquid with ice cubes and lemon floating in it.

'I don't drink,' said Jake.

'In that case you'll be OK with this,' said Johnson, thrusting one of the glasses into his hand. 'Tonic water.'

Jake took the glass and followed her through the crowd to a bench pushed up against one wall. She sat down, and Jake dropped down beside her. The bench was small and it was a tight squeeze, but he was relieved not to be getting on that bike again for another nightmare journey.

'So you're going to tell me where you fit in with all this stuff?' he asked.

'With the hidden library of the Order of Malichea.' Johnson nodded.

Once again, as he heard the words, Jake felt a weird sensation. Did everyone know about this organisation and talk about it so matter-of-factly? Alex Munro had. And now Penny Johnson was talking about it in the same casual tone, as if it was common knowledge. Yet just a few days ago, Jake had never heard of them. And, according to Lauren, their existence was a secret, denied by the scientific establishment. It was certainly covered up by Gareth, if the business in the archives was anything to go by.

'There's an organisation called the Watchers,' said Johnson. Her voice was low, and Jake had to strain to hear what she was saying, especially over the music. 'It was set up originally when the books were buried by the monks in 1497. It was a secret organisation, because the books themselves were secret. I'm sure you know that?'

'Yes,' said Jake. 'With the threat of the books being burned as heretical.'

'Not just the books, the monks as well,' said Johnson.

He leant forward, his face close to hers, as he strained to hear her words.

'The Watchers were composed of people who were trusted by the monks at Glastonbury who hid the

198

books. So – cooks, servants, carpenters, stonemasons, tradespeople. People who worked in the background. The sort no one notices. Their job was to keep watch over the hidden books and make sure no one discovered them by accident, or on purpose. No one except the monks who'd hidden them, that is.'

'Sort of security?' asked Jake.

'Yes. The idea was that they would keep the books safe until the time was right for them to be revealed.'

'But that time never came,' said Jake. 'The plague wiped out the monks.'

'And then came Henry VIII, and then other kings, all of whom wouldn't be sympathetic to these heretical ideas coming out into the open,' said Johnson. 'Even in the twentieth century there were organisations like the Catholic Church with their list of banned books, and others. And all the time the Watchers kept watch over the books, making sure their hiding places remained undisturbed. The job was handed down from generation to generation. Parents to their children. Uncles and aunts to nieces and nephews. They were still ordinary people doing ordinary jobs – nurses, teachers, railway workers, taxi drivers, carpenters, journalists . . .'

'You're a Watcher!' exclaimed Jake, startled. Then hastily he snapped his mouth shut, looking around in alarm in case he'd been overheard. But the *thud thud*

*thud* of the music was too loud for anyone to have heard what they were speaking about.

'Yes.'

'How does it work?' he asked. 'How many of you are there?'

'I don't know,' answered Johnson. 'That's how the Watchers have remained secret for so long. Each book is protected by a small cell of about four people. They don't know the identities of any of the people in the other cells who are guarding the other books. That way, they can't reveal anything other than about their own book.'

'But they know what their particular book is about?' asked Jake.

'No,' said Johnson. 'In those first days, all these people knew was that the books were being hidden to keep them safe, because what was written in them was considered dangerous by the enemies of the abbey. Remember, most of the original Watchers were simple tradespeople who couldn't read or write. Their job was simply to guard them. I inherited the job of watching over the book that was hidden at the fairy-ring site. I was never told what the book was about, only that it had to be protected. Once I heard there were plans to build that new university science block at the site, our cell set to work: raising planning objections, all the usual stuff. When those failed we stirred up the protestors.'

200

'How?'

'Articles in the paper and features on the local TV and radio. Letters of protest. People can be stirred up if you know which buttons to push.'

'And when that failed . . .'

'Then it was a case of keeping a close watch on the site, and – if the book was found – trying to find out where it went, and recover it so it could be hidden again.'

Jake thought about it. The whole thing was so far-fetched. But then, everything that had happened had been too much to believe.

'Who are the other people in your cell?' asked Jake.

Johnson shook her head.

'That's secret,' she said. 'It's only because of what's happened that I've decided to tell you that *I'm* a Watcher. You getting hold of the book. And Pierce Randall.'

He frowned. 'How exactly did you know about my meeting with Alex Munro. And everything else that's happened to me?'

'I'm a Watcher,' said Johnson. 'I'm supposed to keep an eye on the book, and protect it. I wouldn't be much good at that if I didn't know what was going on.'

'So you've been spying on me,' he accused.

'No. We've been watching Pierce Randall as part of our duties.'

'For how long?'

'Ever since they got into the Malichea business.'

The way she said it, with a heavily sarcastic tone, jolted Jake.

'They only want to do good with these sciences,' he pointed out, stung. 'Just like Lauren. Surely that's better than letting all that information lie hidden underground where no one benefits?'

'Is that what Munro told you?' She smiled. 'Yes, he would.'

'You've got a different take on it?'

'Remember the info on that website. Pierce Randall are interested in just two things: money and power. They want to get their hands on these sciences so they can patent them. Can you imagine if you hold the patent on a cure for cancer! You can hold the whole world to ransom; demand any price you want, and people will pay it.'

'That's not true,' said Jake, shaking his head. 'Munro told me they want to stop companies doing that sort of thing. They want to put this information out into the public arena, free, so that everyone benefits.'

'Well, of course that's what he's going to say!' scoffed Johnson. 'You wouldn't be on his side if he told you the truth!'

Jake fell silent. I don't know what to believe, he thought.

'The book mustn't go to Pierce Randall,' said Johnson firmly.

Jake mulled over what she had just said. He looked around him, at the crowd of talking and laughing bikers, his mind numbed by the incessant loud pounding of the music.

'So you're saying that Pierce Randall are behind what's been happening? Carl Parsons and that man being killed in my flat. The attacks on me.'

Johnson looked thoughtful.

'I don't know,' she said. 'My instinct is to say yes, but there are lots of people who'd like to lay their hands on those books and the information that's inside them. Governments, crooks, terrorists, investment banks. Not all of them are on Pierce Randall's client list. But one thing's for sure, whoever it is has used you big time. They used you to get into Hadley Park and get the book out. They obviously thought it would be easier to get it off you afterwards than try to break in themselves.'

'But how have they known what we were up to? We were very careful.'

Johnson shook her head.

'Not that careful, particularly with current surveillance techniques. They can track you just by the signal from your mobile phone, even when you're not using it. You've been followed by hi-tech surveillance ever since you got involved. They've known where you are at any time, who you've met, where you've been.'

'So Lauren and Carl . . .'

'Carl Parsons was a Watcher.'

Jake stared at Johnson.

'What?' he said, dumbfounded.

'That was why he got close to Lauren, as soon as he found out she was looking for the books.'

Jake's mind whirled. Parsons, a Watcher!

'So he was one of your four, your cell, whatever you call it.'

'No,' said Johnson, shaking her head. 'There are some Watchers who float, move around. Sometimes they join a cell for a short while, but generally they go wherever there's news of problems over a book.'

'Sort of troubleshooters?' said Jake.

She nodded.

'Well, it can't have been Pierce Randall who killed him.'

'Why?'

'Lauren gave the book to Parsons so he could hide it. Whoever killed Parsons must have done it for the book. Tonight, Alex Munro asked me to get him the book. If he'd killed Parsons, he'd already have the book in his possession.'

'Not necessarily,' countered Johnson. 'Maybe Parsons was killed before they could get him to give them the book.'

She looked at her watch.

'You need to go,' she said. 'If you're out of that apartment too long, they'll get suspicious.' She gave him a firm look. 'It wouldn't be wise for you to tell them you were with me. I suspect they know I'm a Watcher.'

'Don't worry, I'll lie,' said Jake. He gave a rueful sigh. 'It goes with being a press officer.'

'Maybe,' agreed Johnson, 'but I don't think you're very good at it. Lying, I mean.'

She stood up, and Jake felt a burst of fear at getting back on her motorbike.

'That's OK,' he said quickly. 'There's no need to take me back to the apartment. I can get a cab there.'

She grinned. 'The ride scared you that much, huh?'

'No,' protested Jake indignantly.

Johnson laughed. 'Like I said, you're a useless liar.'

# Chapter 23

Jake caught a cab back to the apartment block. It was midnight by the time he got in. He tried Lauren's phone again, but as before, all he got was her voice-mail message. He hung up. All he wanted to do was crawl into bed and sleep. But his mind wouldn't let him. Every time he closed his eyes, the images of the day came back to him: the two men threatening him in the street; the dead man on the floor of his flat; the image of Lauren running away on CCTV; the story on the TV news of Lauren accused of the murder of Carl Parsons; Alex Munro at Pierce Randall; Penny Johnson and her terrifying motorbike. And all in one day. It was enough for a lifetime.

The sound of the doorbell buzzing woke him. He looked at the bedside clock, and jerked up with a start. 8.45!

He pulled on his jeans and hurried barefoot to the door and unlocked it. Sue Clark stared at him, at the fact that he was still undressed. And I bet I stink of booze from that bikers' bar, Jake thought to himself ruefully.

'You were supposed to be ready,' she snapped at him, her tone curt and very disapproving.

'I'm sorry,' he said. 'I overslept. It was a tough day yesterday . . .'

'Tell me later,' she ordered. 'Take a shower and get dressed.'

As Jake hurried to the bathroom, he wondered if he should ask if there would be time to get some breakfast, but he could tell by Clark's face that she wouldn't be sympathetic.

In the car on the way to the police station, Clark asked him, 'Where did you go last night? The concierge said you went out.'

'Er . . . just out for a walk.'

'Why? We put you in the apartment to keep you safe.'

'Because I needed to clear my head.' Johnson says I'm a useless liar, mused Jake. Let's hope I can persuade Clark to believe me. 'Like I say, it had been a really rough day. I sat inside the apartment and felt the walls closing in on me. I had to get out and think.'

Clark didn't even look at him. She doesn't believe me, he thought. She's going to ask me who I met.

207

But instead, the lawyer simply said, 'You won't have that problem any more. You should be able to go back to your flat after we've finished at the police station.'

Jake frowned. 'You sure it's going to be that easy? They seemed pretty sure I'm the one who killed that man.'

'Just leave it to me,' said Clark. 'I do the talking. You keep your mouth shut unless I tell you that you can speak. Got that?'

'Got it,' he said meekly.

At the police station, everything went exactly as Sue Clark had said it would. It was almost as if she and Detective Inspector Edgar had rehearsed their lines beforehand. By ten thirty, Jake and Clark were leaving the police station – after he'd signed a declaration that he wouldn't be leaving the country without first checking with the police.

'OK,' said Clark. 'That's it, for the moment. You're free, providing you don't do anything stupid. Like break into another research establishment.' Then she added, pointedly, 'Or conceal evidence.'

'What sort of evidence?' asked Jake.

'Lauren Graham,' said Clark. 'If she gets in touch with you.'

'You're telling me I should tell the police if I hear from her?'

208

'No,' said Clark, shaking her head. 'You contact me. If I'm not available, you contact Mr Munro direct, or anyone else at Pierce Randall.' She gave him a card. 'These are the other numbers you'll need. They'll tell you what to do.' She gestured at the car that had pulled up in the car park. Once again, Keith was at the wheel. 'Are you going back to your flat? I can drop you off.'

Jake thought about negotiating public transport: buses or underground trains, or even taxis, and realised he still felt very vulnerable.

'Yes, please,' he said.

They drove in silence for most of the way, with Clark texting busily beside him, but as they neared his flats she said, 'Mr Munro will be in touch with you very shortly.'

'Oh?'

'About the missing books,' she said. 'He is sure you will be able to help us. Let me assure you, it will be a relationship that could be very advantageous to you. After all, I can imagine that your job situation must be a bit precarious at the moment.'

Gareth! The realisation hit Jake hard. With everything that had gone on – being attacked by the duo, finding the dead man in his flat, Parsons being murdered and Lauren on the run – all that had pushed what had happened at work the previous morning out of his mind. He had to get in touch with Gareth and come up with some explanation. But what could he say? *I thought you were trying to kill me?*

'We are experts at employment law,' said Clark. 'We can negotiate a very good settlement for you, if your employers try to sack you, or you want to leave.'

'Thanks,' said Jake, awkwardly.

'I suggest we meet later today to discuss the best way to deal with your current employers.' She checked her planner. 'I've got a full programme, but I can do five o'clock, if that's good for you?'

Pierce Randall are taking over my life, he thought. I don't want this! I want to be free. I want things to be like they were, only with me and Lauren happy and together. But he heard himself say numbly, 'OK.'

'Five it is,' she said, and she tapped in the appointment on her planner. 'I'll see you at Pierce Randall's offices. Just give your name at reception.'

The car had arrived outside Jake's flats.

'Five it is,' he said, as he opened the door. 'And, thank you.'

'All part of the Pierce Randall service,' said Clark. 'I'll see you later.'

Jake watched the car move away, then he turned to look at his small block of flats. Home! He was free! He had no intention of going back to Pierce Randall at five, or any other time. At least, not until he'd got his head together and sorted out what was going on, and whom he could trust. And work out where the danger he was facing was coming from.

He had to get away. Out of sight, somewhere safe. But where?

He suddenly realised he hadn't switched his mobile on. He'd turned it off while he was being interviewed at the police station, and then kept it switched off while he was in the car. He turned it on, and saw he had a message: a missed call. When he saw the number his heart gave a leap. Lauren had called! He rang her number immediately. She answered at the first ring.

'Jake!' Her voice sounded nervous, frightened. But then, considering what she must have been through, that wasn't surprising.

'Lauren! Where are you?'

'I can't tell you, in case they're listening in.'

'What happened with Carl?'

'Oh, Jake, it was horrible!' Her words came tumbling out. 'I changed my mind.'

'About what?'

'About letting him have the book to look after. It was my project, I should be the one to take care of it. But when I said this to Carl, he got upset and tried to force me to give it to him.'

'Because he was a Watcher,' said Jake.

'A what?' asked Lauren, her tone bewildered.

211

'They were – are – an organisation set up to watch over the books. Take care of them. Protect them.'

'No. He wanted it because he'd arranged to sell it to someone.'

'To sell it?!' Jake repeated, shocked.

'Yes. When I wouldn't hand over the book to him, he . . .' she hesitated, 'he picked up a knife and threatened me with it. I'd never seen him like that before. He was going on about how much money there was at stake. Millions! It wasn't the Carl I knew. He was frightening.'

'So he used us to get the book for him?'

'Yes!' From her voice, Jake could tell she was crying now. 'Anyway, he came at me and . . . we struggled . . . and then . . . I grabbed at his wrist to try and stop him cutting me with the knife, and . . .' Over the phone, Jake heard her take a series of deep breaths.

'There's no need to say it.'

'There is,' she said. 'It was an accident. We were struggling, and then suddenly his body went limp and he fell to the floor, moaning. That's when I saw the handle of the knife sticking out of his chest.'

People could be listening, thought Jake. You've just confessed to killing someone! But it was self-defence. Manslaughter. Not even manslaughter. An accident. An accident and self-defence. She'd need a good lawyer. Pierce Randall.

I'll be seeing them at five o'clock after all, he decided.

'Why didn't you phone me after it happened?' he asked, hurt.

'I didn't want to phone anyone. I thought they might be bugging our phones, tracing me. But right now, I don't know what to do or who to turn to. You're the only one I can trust, apart from Robert. And Robert doesn't know what's been going on.'

'We have to meet,' said Jake.

'No,' said Lauren. 'They'll be watching you. If we meet, they'll get me.'

'There's this firm of lawyers called Pierce Randall,' he said. 'They helped me. They'll help you. Protect you. Come with me to meet them.'

'No,' said Lauren.

'Who was Carl going to sell the book to?' he asked.

'I don't know,' she answered.

'Whoever it was, if they get in touch with you, give them the book,' said Jake. 'That's all they want. Give them the book and they'll stop.'

'No!' said Lauren. 'Not after all this! I killed some-one I cared for, who I thought cared for me! If I just hand it over, what's all this been about?'

'It doesn't matter what it's been about,' insisted Jake. 'What matters is you stay alive. There'll be other books. Give them this one.'

There was a pause, then Lauren said, 'I haven't got it. I've put it somewhere safe.'

'Where?'

'I have to go,' said Lauren. 'Go home, Jake. Go home. Stay safe.'

Then the line went dead. He dialled her number, but all he got was the usual mechanical voice informing him that 'This person's phone is switched off', and telling him to leave a message.

He headed into his block of flats, and shuddered as he remembered the last time he'd walked in. The fear and panic he'd fought to keep under control as he entered his flat, and the shock at finding the dead man's body. He knew he ought to feel as apprehensive about going back, but he didn't. He felt battered and exhausted. If anyone leapt out at him now, he'd quite likely just say to them, 'I haven't got the book. I don't know where it is. Now can you please leave?'

There was no one waiting for him on the stairs, nor on the landing outside his flat. The 'scene of crime' tape he'd presumed the police had fixed across his flat door had gone. Everything looked the same as before.

He turned his key in the lock, pushed the door open, and found himself treading on the post: junk mail, a few envelopes with what looked like bills, and a jiffy bag.

He picked up the jiffy bag, and felt his heart pound as he recognised Lauren's writing on it. It couldn't be. . . !

He opened the jiffy bag. Inside was the book they'd taken from the research lab. The one everyone was looking for. The one over which people had died. And now he was holding it in his hands.

# Chapter 24

Jake sat in his living room, the book on the table in front of him. That was why Lauren had stressed for him to go home. She'd sent the book to the only place she thought was safe.

Jake's mind was in a whirl. What should he do with it? Give it to Pierce Randall and let them take it into safe keeping? Give it to Penny Johnson? But how would either of those actions help Lauren?

He reached out and touched it, being careful not to disturb it too much in case it fell open, just in case there were any fungal spores still hidden among the pages. Not that it looked as if that would happen easily – it now had an elastic band holding it shut – but Jake was still cautious after what he'd seen happen before.

The book was encased in what looked to be a sort of oilskin or leather, black in colour. A symbol was embossed into the material. It was the same symbol Lauren had

216

on her laptop, the seal of the Order of Malichea. And, etched into the material just beneath the symbol were the Roman numerals CCCLXVII. So this was book number 367, which meant there were at least another 366 books out there from the secret library, hidden.

I have to hang on to this book, Jake told himself. I have to hang on to it until I find out who's chasing Lauren, and use it to stop them. I'll give it to them to keep her safe, whether she wants me to or not. As he'd said to Lauren, there'd be other books to find; but there was only one Lauren. He had to protect her.

He got up and began pacing the room – he felt useless sitting down. He needed to be *doing* something. But what? As he walked past his window, he looked out, and saw a man leaning against a low wall on the other side of the street, reading a newspaper. Warning bells went off in Jake's head. He was sure he'd noticed that same man when he'd arrived home, in the same place, by the low wall on the other side of the road opposite the entrance to his flats.

OK, he could be just a man waiting for someone. But Jake was sure he wasn't. He studied the man. Tall. Nothing special about him. Wearing jeans, a casual jacket and trainers. And his attention didn't seem to be completely on the paper he was holding. Every now and then the man's eyes darted towards the front of Jake's block of flats, and the entrance.

They've been watching for me, waiting for me to come back. And now he's seen me come in, my guess is he's phoned the people he's working with and let them know I'm here.

Who is he? Who are they? The Watchers? Pierce Randall? It was obvious that Sue Clark didn't believe him when he'd said he'd been for a walk the night before.

Perhaps the man was working for the people who Carl Parsons had been going to sell the book to? Or maybe he was working for Gareth? After all, Gareth was in this up to his neck.

Or perhaps it was a completely different organisation. What was it Penny Johnson had said: *there are lots of people who'd like to lay their hands on those books and the information that's inside them. Governments, crooks, terrorists, investment banks.* Which were these: the man watching his flat and his associates?

As Jake watched, a car pulled up beside the man. The man put his newspaper away, went to the car and said something to the driver. The car doors opened and two men got out. One of them looked up towards Jake's flat, and Jake just managed to duck to one side to avoid being seen.

They're coming for me! he thought. I have to call for help!

But who could he call? Whoever it was, they wouldn't be here before those men got to his flat. And locking his flat door and refusing to let them in wouldn't help. They'd got in before without trouble, when that man had been killed. And, looking at these men, he was sure that they'd just crash his door in anyway.

He chanced a look out of his window. The two men had gone to the boot of the car and were taking something out of it. As the boot lid slammed down, Jake saw that one of the men was now carrying a long dark holdall. It could be anything: a shotgun, a sledge-hammer to batter down his door.

Jake picked up the book and stuffed it into his jacket pocket, then he ran for the front door. He opened it and banged on the door of the flat opposite, Mrs O'Brien. As the door opened and Mrs O'Brien peered out, Jake pushed against the door, but the security chain held it firmly and stopped it from opening.

'Yes?' Mrs O'Brien asked curtly, wariness and suspicion showing clearly on her face.

'Mrs O'Brien, please let me in!' begged Jake. 'It's urgent!'

'Why?' demanded Mrs O'Brien. She was about fifty and regarded everything with suspicion, especially her neighbours, and in particular a young neighbour like Jake.

'Please!!! It's a matter of life or death!'

Mrs O'Brien glared back at him. 'You expect me to let you in, after what happened? A dead man in your flat!'

'I didn't do it! That wasn't me!' Jake appealed to her. 'If I had, they wouldn't have let me go!'

Below, he heard the door from the street open.

'Please, Mrs O'Brien, I promise you, I'm innocent! But I need your help, desperately.'

Mrs O'Brien hesitated, then very deliberately she pushed the door shut in his face.

Oh God, I'm dead! thought Jake. He could hear the men's footsteps coming up the stairs.

Then the door opened again, released from the security chain, and Jake fell gratefully into her flat.

Mrs O'Brien shut the door again and refixed the chain in its place.

'What's going on?' she demanded sternly. 'That dead man in your flat. The police arrested you . . .'

'I didn't do it!' Jake told her frantically. 'Someone tried to frame me! But the police let me go. And now the people who tried to frame me are here!'

Mrs O'Brien looked at him, shocked.

'Here?'

Jake nodded. 'They're coming to my flat.'

Mrs O'Brien went towards the phone. 'We'll call the police.'

'No!' blurted out Jake. He didn't want to be found with the book on him. They'd take it off him, and it was the only thing he had that could help Lauren.

From outside, he heard voices. The men were talking, calmly and quietly, loud enough for him to hear them, although not what they were saying. There had been no sounds of his door being broken open, nor his doorbell ringing. He guessed they must have got hold of the keys to his flat and let themselves in.

Mrs O'Brien gave Jake a glare.

'If there are people like that out there, I'm phoning the police, whether you like it or not!' she told him firmly.

She picked up the phone and was about to dial, when there was a knocking at her door.

'It's them!' Jake said, horrified.

'Police!' called a voice through the door. 'Open up, please!'

Mrs O'Brien looked at Jake, a bewildered expression on her face.

'They say they're police,' she said.

'They're lying,' said Jake urgently. 'Ask to see their identification.'

'I always do,' said Mrs O'Brien. She put the phone down and called out, 'All right! I'm coming!'

'No!' called Jake, but Mrs O'Brien had already disappeared into the small hallway of her flat. Frantically, Jake looked around. He was trapped!

He heard the door open and then Mrs O'Brien say, 'Let me see your identification.'

Then a male voice said, 'Certainly.'

Of course they'd have police ID cards, thought Jake. They'd have everything they needed.

'Do you know a Mr Jake Wells, your neighbour?' asked the voice.

'Why?' asked Mrs O'Brien.

'We have reason to believe he may be hiding in one of the other flats in this block . . .'

She's going to let them in! realised Jake with a shock. Of course she is. She thinks they're police. And they'll take me away and find the book, and kill me.

And then he remembered the fire escape which served the whole block, with escape doors from the flats at the back. Mrs O'Brien's flat was at the back.

As Jake heard Mrs O'Brien saying, 'He's here all right. I knew something was up,' and the sound of the security chain being unfixed, he was already running into the kitchen. Yes, there was the fire-exit door. He rushed to it, pushed it, and almost fell out on to the fire escape. And then he was running, clattering down the metal steps.

He heard a shout behind him, a man calling, 'Stop him!' Then the sounds of running feet. A man appeared at the bottom of the fire escape, the same man who'd been keeping watch. The man reached into his jacket and started to pull something out, but he never made it. Jake jumped, kicking out with his foot as he did so, and caught the man full in the face. The man stumbled, and fell back, clutching his face. Jake didn't wait to see what the man had been pulling from his jacket: a knife or a gun or some other sort of weapon.

Jake ran. His lungs were full to bursting as he reached the pavement and his legs seemed as if they were going to fail him and he would fall, but he could hear the boots close behind him and a voice shout, 'Get the car!'

A car! He'd never be able to outrun a car!

Only one set of running boots was behind him now; the other had gone to get the car. Then Jake saw a bike, a kid's mountain bike, leaning against a wall. He grabbed it and carried on running with it, jumped on it and started pedalling, faster and faster, turning rapidly left into one of the side walkways that ran through to the next street. It went between two blocks of flats and had bollards across it to stop cars getting through.

He cycled faster, picking up speed, and he could hear the running boots behind him recede. He did another sharp turn, and another, into a maze of narrow alleyways that he knew no car could get down, and then he cycled as fast as he could until he reached a main road, busy with pedestrians and traffic. He abandoned the bike, and disappeared into a shopping mall, pushing his way through a crowd of shoppers, until he was gone from sight of the main street.

He'd done it! He'd got away! But now what? Who were those men? And where could he go now?

# Chapter 25

He was barely inside the shopping mall when his mobile rang. The voice on the phone was a man's, very coldly businesslike.

'You have the book. We have Ms Graham. Deliver the book to us, or Ms Graham will die.'

Jake felt sick. They had Lauren.

'Did you hear what I said?' demanded the voice.

'How do I know you've got her?' asked Jake.

'Wait.'

There was a pause, then Lauren's voice was heard saying. 'Jake . . .' The phone was snatched away from her; but not before Jake had heard her fear and desperation in that one word.

'OK,' he said. 'An exchange. When and where?'

'We will contact you and give you the location,' said the voice. 'But if you make contact with the authorities or anyone else, and bring them with you, she will die.'

225

'No authorities,' promised Jake.

'And keep your lawyers out of this,' added the voice. 'If you contact them, she will die.'

'No lawyers,' Jake assured the man.

'Good,' said the voice. 'We understand one another. We will phone you and tell you the location for the exchange.'

The phone went dead.

Who were they? thought Jake. One thing was for sure, it wasn't Pierce Randall. The voice on the phone had made the point that Jake wasn't to contact the lawyers. Unless it was a double bluff on Pierce Randall's part: getting the book back, but keeping Jake on their side for the future.

Jake was certain it wasn't the Watchers. He'd met Penny Johnson, and these sorts of death threats weren't their style, despite Carl Parsons attacking Lauren. He also felt the phone call ruled Gareth out from being behind Lauren's kidnapping. He'd been told not to go to the authorities. Well, Gareth *was* the authorities.

But he needed *someone* with him if he was to make sure Lauren, and himself, came out of this alive once the book had been handed over.

Robert looked out of his front door at Jake, and then past him into the street.

'Where's Lauren?' he asked suspiciously.

'She's been kidnapped,' said Jake.

Robert's mouth dropped open, shocked. Then he clamped it shut again, his eyes searching Jake's face.

'What?! Who by?'

'I don't know, but they've threatened to kill her,' said Jake.

Robert's expression turned to the kind that must have struck terror into his opponents on the rugby field.

'Over my dead body!' he snarled.

'I hoped you'd say that,' said Jake.

Jake went in and Robert shut the door and followed him into the ultra-neat living room.

'This is about the books?' Robert asked.

Jake nodded, and then filled him in on what had been happening over the last few days, including the accidental stabbing of Parsons, and Lauren posting the book to him. Jake took the book out and showed it to him. Robert reached out tentatively and took the book from him, turning it over in his huge hands, studying it, the dark leather-like material that encased it, and the symbol of Malichea etched into it. He didn't attempt to open it. Instead, he handed it back to Jake, who slipped it into his jacket pocket.

'The trouble is, they know I've got it,' Jake told Robert.

'How?'

Jake sighed.

'They may have forced Lauren to tell them what she did with it,' he said unhappily.

Robert's face darkened and he smashed a huge fist against the nearest wall at the thought of Lauren being tortured for the information.

'Anyway, they said they'd hand her over if I give them the book,' said Jake. 'They're going to phone me to tell me where the exchange is to take place.'

'And you want me to go with you.'

It wasn't a question, it was a statement. Robert was coming with Jake.

'Yes,' agreed Jake. 'I don't trust them. The trouble is, they said that if I bring along the authorities, or anyone else, they'll kill her. So I don't know how we're going to play this. I don't think two of us will be enough to handle them; but if we bring any more, it could blow the whole thing.'

Robert was silent, thinking it over.

'You've no idea where the exchange is going to be?'

'No.'

Just then, Jake's mobile rang. He put his finger to his lips to urge Robert to keep quiet, then answered it.

'Jake Wells,' he said.

'Forty-three Wharf Road North, Paddington,' snapped a voice. 'Fifty minutes.'

'I can't possibly get there in fifty minutes . . .' Jake

began. But he was speaking to empty air. The caller had hung up.

He looked at Robert.

'Forty-three . . .' he began.

'I heard,' said Robert. He'd grabbed a jacket and was already hurrying towards the front door.

# Chapter 26

Fifty minutes. Why fifty minutes? The specific time worried Jake. They must have known where I was, he thought. From Baron's Court to Paddington. There was no way they'd be able to make the journey in fifty minutes in Robert's battered old van, certainly not with congestion in central London as bad as it was. The underground was possible, but with delays happening constantly, and changes to be made, and then looking for Wharf Road North on foot, fifty minutes became very doubtful. So it had to be a taxi, the only other vehicle that could use bus lanes and hopefully get through the traffic, and be able to take them right to their destination.

Jake and Robert raced to the taxi rank at the High Road, and very shortly they were in the back of a cab heading towards central London.

In the cab, Jake expressed his concern that the kidnappers knew where he'd been when they phoned.

'It's that business of fifty minutes. This way, we can just do it in fifty minutes. If I'd been further out, we'd never make it there in time.'

'And you think if you'd been nearer, they'd have given you less time to get there. Say, twenty minutes if you'd been at Euston?'

'Exactly.' Jake nodded. 'They're watching me.' Then the realisation hit him as he remembered what Penny Johnson had said. 'No, they're *tracking* me!' He pulled out his mobile phone. 'Someone told me that both Lauren and I have been tracked by the signals from our mobile phones. Even when they're switched off they give out a signal.'

'This is someone with very powerful and sophisticated tracking equipment,' grunted Robert.

'It is,' said Jake. 'Which means, if they know about you, they'll know you're with me.'

Robert scowled.

'Damn!' he burst out. Then he leant forward and tapped on the glass between them and the driver. 'Pull over!' he ordered.

The cab driver immediately pulled over to the kerb.

'Wait here,' commanded Robert.

He got out of the cab and walked along the kerb until he came to a drain, where he dropped his mobile phone. Then he walked back to the cab, got in, and ordered the driver to carry on. Robert looked at Jake

231

and gave a wry smile. 'That was a good phone as well,' he said.

'Someone will find it,' said Jake. 'One of the sewer workers. You might end up with phone bills for calls to Australia.'

Robert shook his head. 'It's pay as you go,' he said. 'Anyway, from now on they'll think I've left you and you're on your own. So, what's the plan?'

'To be honest, I don't have one,' admitted Jake. 'I just thought we'd have more chance of getting Lauren out of this alive if there was more than just me.'

Robert looked at him, his expression doubtful. 'That's not much of a plan!'

'No, it isn't,' agreed Jake with a sigh.

'And we don't have anything to protect ourselves with,' pointed out Robert. 'No weapons or body armour of any sort. And these people are quite likely armed to the teeth, and there'll be loads of them.'

'Yes,' sighed Jake gloomily. 'You don't have to come in with me, Robert. Like you say, it's a loser. All we can hope is they're true to their word. If they're not, there's not much the two of us can do about it.'

'You give up easily,' muttered Robert disapprovingly.

'I'm not giving up,' protested Jake. 'I'm just saying there's no need for both of us to . . .' He hesitated.

'Get killed?' asked Robert.

'Well, I wasn't going to exactly say that,' said Jake awkwardly.

'No one kills me,' stated Robert firmly. 'I play rugby.'

'But not against bullets.'

'We don't *know* they've got guns.'

'They're some sort of gangsters,' countered Jake. 'They're bound to have guns.'

'But they won't use them,' said Robert. 'Not if we bluff them.'

'Bluff them? How?'

'I don't know,' admitted Robert. 'But we'll think of something.'

He looked at his watch, and then at the area they were entering. 'And we'd better do it fast,' he said. 'We're just coming to Paddington Station.'

As the taxi turned off the main road past Paddington Station, and then into Wharf Road North, Jake racked his brains for a scheme to bluff their unknown enemies with. Telling them the police were outside wouldn't help – they'd said they'd kill Lauren if he brought the police in.

The taxi crawled along the Wharf Road. It appeared to be filled with warehouses and storage companies. They pulled up outside number forty-three, a warehouse which looked like it hadn't been occupied for some time.

'This is it,' said Jake.

He felt a knot of nervousness in his stomach as he and Robert got out of the taxi and he paid the driver.

'Any plan yet?' asked Robert.

'Yes and no,' said Jake. 'I think I go in alone. You see if you can creep in and hide somewhere and watch, and make a move if things look bad. After all, if that phone thing of yours worked, they won't know you're here.' Jake took his mobile phone and handed it to Robert. 'Just in case things do go bad, you can phone nine-nine-nine.'

Robert hesitated and seemed about to reject the phone. Then he took it from Jake and slipped it into his pocket.

'Thanks,' he said. He turned to Jake. 'I was wrong about you,' he said gruffly. 'I thought you were no good and using Lauren. You really care for her, don't you?'

'Yes,' said Jake. 'I love her. I was stupid with the way I behaved at that wedding, and I've regretted it every day since. I want to make things right again.'

'You already have done,' said Robert. 'Whatever happens.' He looked towards the abandoned warehouse. 'Ready?'

'No,' admitted Jake. 'I feel sick, I feel scared.' He took a deep breath. 'But I'm as ready as I'll ever be. So let's do it.'

# Chapter 27

Jake walked across the patch of tarmac towards the warehouse. He guessed that once there would have been lorries and cars parked here. Now it seemed to be used as a dumping ground for rubbish. Broken wooden pallets lay around, where they had been dropped or thrown. Black bags filled with litter had just been dumped and had split, with paper and other rubbish spilling out.

There'll be rats, thought Jake. He remembered reading somewhere that in London you were never more than three metres from a rat. That usually meant that the rat was underground, below you, but in cases like this he guessed the rats were living in the old warehouse, scavenging and breeding. He was sure he saw a movement among the piles of torn litter bins. Jake hated rats. The fact of them sent a shiver up his spine. They could get anywhere, through the most incredibly narrow gaps. And their teeth were so sharp they could gnaw through porcelain. He'd heard tales of them chewing their way through a toilet bowl to get into a flat to scavenge for food.

Most of the doors into the building were shut with metal bars locked down across them, but one door was slightly ajar. That's the way they want me to go in, thought Jake.

He wondered where Robert was. Robert had gone off to the far side of the building, looking for a window or an opening so he could creep in unnoticed. Even if he did manage to get in unseen, it only gave them a force of two. Two unarmed amateurs against armed and fully prepared professionals.

Jake reached the door and pushed it gently. It swung open. From inside, there was a dim light glowing. He wondered where they'd be. Waiting for him just inside the door, ready to pounce on him? He reached down and picked up a nearby plastic bag filled with litter that had been left lying near the doorway, and then tossed it through the door opening.

Nothing happened. No one shot at the bag, or jumped on it. But then, these people were professionals. Jake guessed they knew what they were doing.

He hesitated, then took a deep breath, and walked in through the doorway, into the warehouse.

It wasn't empty. It may have been disused, but it was still stacked with machinery and crates, all covered with dust and cobwebs. It had been a very long time since this place had been active.

'Welcome, Mr Wells!' boomed a voice. 'We are glad you could join us! Come forward!'

'I'm armed!' called out Jake in warning.

There was a chuckle, then the voice said, 'We think that unlikely, Mr Wells. I doubt if you've ever handled a gun, before or now.'

'I don't need a gun!' called back Jake. He took a deep breath, then tried his bluff. 'I've wired myself with explosives under my clothes. If you shoot me, I'll blow up and we'll all be killed.' There, thought Jake. I've come up with a plan. Mad, perhaps, but it's still a plan.

There was a pause, then the voice laughed again.

'Really, Mr Wells . . .'

But Jake was sure this time the laugh wasn't as confident.

'Since this started I've met some dodgy people,' called Jake. 'Believe me, I'm wired to blow up.'

There was a pause, then the voice asked, 'You have the book with you?'

'Yes,' called Jake. 'And if you shoot me and I blow up, the book goes up in flames.'

'There is no need for that,' said the voice. 'Come forward. With your hands above your head, please.'

Jake hesitated, then edged slowly forward, hands raised, expecting at any moment a shot to ring out.

None came. Had they bought his bluff? Penny Johnson had said he was a useless liar. He hoped this would prove her wrong.

There was a clearing in the centre of the warehouse. As Jake moved slowly into the clearing, he looked around at the piles of crates stacked up and the large, idle machines; all offered places where these people could be hiding, guns trained on him.

'Where's Lauren?' he called.

There was the sound of scuffling, and then two men appeared from behind a pile of crates. They wore black balaclava helmets covering their faces. Both of them held pistols which they pointed at Jake. There was more scuffling, then Lauren appeared, pushed forward by a third man, his face also covered with a balaclava. Her hands were tied behind her back and there was tape across her mouth.

'Take the tape off,' instructed Jake.

There was a pause, then the voice said, 'You are in no position to make demands.'

'Take the tape off!' snapped Jake, his voice sounding firmer this time. He was scared, he knew he was quite likely going to die, but there was no way he was going to make it easy for these people.

He wondered where the person who was speaking was hiding. The voice had an echo to it, like it was being amplified. Maybe the person behind the voice wasn't even here in the warehouse, but somewhere else, watching it all on CCTV.

'Remove the tape,' ordered the voice, and one of the men reached out and ripped the tape off. Lauren uttered a small cry of pain as it was torn away.

'Are you OK?' asked Jake.

'Yes,' she said. Her voice sounded distant, faint. Jake noticed that she was being held up by the third man, and wondered if she'd been drugged.

Suddenly, there was a commotion from further inside the warehouse, raised voices, the sound of fists hitting. The two men near Lauren swung round, guns pointing, while the man holding Lauren let her go and pulled out a gun himself. Lauren swayed and crumpled to the ground. Jake started to rush towards her, but one of the men swung his gun to point directly at Jake, and the voice called out warningly, 'Stay where you are, Mr Wells!'

Then two more men appeared, dragging the figure of Robert along with them. Robert struggled in their grasp, until one of the men near Lauren walked over to him and hit him in the face with his gun. Robert swayed, but carried on struggling and shouting, and the man hit him again, harder this time, and Robert sagged and fell to the ground.

'You were told to come alone,' said the amplified voice coldly.

'I didn't trust you,' said Jake. 'And he's not armed. Unlike me.'

'How many more people have you got out there?' asked the voice.

'Wouldn't you like to know?' said Jake, doing his best to appear confident by putting on a mocking tone.

'Enough!' snapped the voice. 'Hand over the book!'

'Not until you release them.'

'You are stupid if you think some kind of stand-off will work here,' said the voice. 'You are out-numbered.'

'I'm also wired to explode, and I can blow me and the book to bits,' Jake reminded him.

'I don't believe you,' said the voice.

Jake shrugged. 'That's up to you,' he said. 'Come on, you said this was an exchange. So let's exchange. Let them go, and I'll put the book down on the floor here.'

'How do we know you even have the book on you?'

Jake hesitated a second, then reached into his pocket, took the book out and held it up.

'Here it is,' he said.

'It could be a fake,' said the voice.

'So let them go and I'll stay here while you check it, as security.'

There was pause, then the voice said, 'Show us the explosives.'

'What?' asked Jake.

'These explosives you claim to have wired ready to go off. Show them to us.'

Jake shook his head.

'They're right under my clothes, next to my skin. If you think I'm going to start undressing and give you the chance to rush me . . .'

'I don't believe you.'

Jake shrugged again.

'Like I said, that's up to you. But look at it this way, you'll be left with me and the book. If I'm lying, you've lost nothing.'

There was a longer pause, then the voice instructed the armed men, 'Release the girl and the other man. Take them outside and let them go.'

Jake noticed that Robert was now sitting up, rubbing his head, dazed and hurt, but conscious.

'I don't hand over the book until I see your men come back in afterwards,' warned Jake.

'Very well. When you have taken the woman and the man outside, come back in.'

Two of the armed men went to Lauren and Robert and lifted them off the ground, and then helped them towards the warehouse door.

Don't try anything, Robert, thought Jake desperately. This is your one chance to get away from here safely.

Lauren and Robert both stumbled as they walked, but they kept moving. As they passed, Lauren threw a helpless and desperate look at Jake. He forced a smile at her. 'It's OK,' he said. 'I know what I'm doing. Go.'

One of the armed men took her by the arm and urged her forward. Jake watched as the four disappeared out of sight around the stacked crates. All this time he stood, the book held in his hand, so the kidnappers could see it.

*Please believe me*, he prayed silently. Please believe that beneath my clothes I'm loaded with explosives and detonators.

There was a wait of what seemed like an eternity, though it was possibly less than a minute. Then the two armed men returned, alone.

'Have they gone?' asked the voice.

One of the masked men nodded.

'Good,' said the voice. 'Now, Mr Wells, the book.'

Jake nodded and laid the book down on the ground.

'Step away from it,' ordered the voice.

Jake stepped back from the book. One of the masked men went to the book and picked it up, examined the seal on the cover, and then raised one hand with his thumb sticking up to confirm it was the book. He took the book and disappeared out of sight behind one of the stacks of crates.

'OK,' said Jake. 'So, I guess that's our business done.'

'Not quite,' said the voice. 'You surely didn't believe we could let you go. We don't know how much you know.'

'I don't know anything about you,' said Jake.

'No, but Ms Graham does,' said the voice. 'She saw our people when they took her. She can describe them.'

A chill went through Jake.

'But . . .' he began.

The voice chuckled. 'I hate to disillusion you, Mr Wells, but I have been known to tell lies. One was that we would release your friends.'

'But your men took them outside! And then they came back!'

'After they'd handed them over to our other operatives who were waiting outside, as back-up.'

There was a scuffling sound from the door, and Jake saw Lauren and Robert being pushed along. This time both had tape fixed firmly across their mouths to stop them warning him, and their hands were behind their backs.

The men shoved them both hard, and Lauren and Robert stumbled forward, crashing into Jake. The three of them stood, recovering and unsteady. Lauren looked at Jake, an apology in her eyes. The armed men had now withdrawn to take cover behind the stacks of crates.

'So, Mr Wells, feel free to blow yourself and your friends up,' said the voice. 'If you don't, then my men will shoot all three of you. You have three seconds. One . . . two . . .'

# Chapter 28

Jake began to run for the exit, grabbing hold of Lauren as he did and hauling her towards it. He heard the deafening sound of gunfire burst out, smelt the burning of metal as bullets tore into wood and the ground around them, chips of concrete flying up. He was aware that Robert was with them, and then, out of the corner of his eye, he saw Robert collapse and tumble.

He pushed Lauren harder, aiming for the door, but as they turned the corner of the stacked crates they ran into a wall of men dressed from head to foot in black pointing automatic rifles at them.

We're dead! thought Jake.

'Down!' barked one of the men. Jake and Lauren found themselves grabbed and forced face down on the ground.

Meanwhile, the sound of gunfire continued behind them, punctuated with screams and yells of pain.

They're not going to kill us, Jake realised. They're here to rescue us!

Suddenly, a voice was heard shouting, 'Cease fire!'

Jake started to lift his head, but a boot was placed on his back, pushing him down again.

'Stay down!' growled a voice.

He lay flat, his face pressed against the dirty cold concrete floor. He was able to see Lauren next to him, still gagged with the tape, but alive.

After the gunfire stopped, the warehouse had an eerie echo. The only sound was that of heavy boots stomping around. Then Jake was aware of more footsteps, quieter ones, approaching. They stopped by him. He twisted his head and saw a pair of shiny black leather shoes close by him.

'All correct, sir!' barked a voice.

'Excellent,' said a calm voice. Gareth!

Ignoring the boots near him, ready to push him back down, Jake looked up, and saw Gareth smiling down at him, with that same smile which was meant to ooze sincerity, but now chilled Jake to the core.

'Well, well, Jake,' said Gareth, his tone gently chiding. 'You do get yourself in some difficult situations.'

It was about an hour later. Jake and Lauren were sitting at a table in a basement room. Security cameras were fixed to all the walls, pointed at them. Jake guessed there were microphones installed as well, recording everything that was said. It was less obvious than his experience at the hands of Detective Inspector Edgar, but this was an interrogation room, nevertheless. Jake had guessed where they'd been headed as the car had brought them towards the large building on the banks of the Thames. MI6 HQ. He'd seen it often enough on his way to work at the Department of Science. He'd heard it given other names. The official address was 85 Albert Embankment, but it was also known within Civil Service circles as Spook Centre, Legoland, and Babylon-on-Thames because of the design of the building, which looked like a massive ziggurat from ancient Babylon when seen from the river. Viewed from land, it looked just like any other huge building in London. It was a building Jake had never thought he'd see the inside of. And now, here he was in an interrogation room somewhere deep in its basement.

Tough-looking men stood around the room, keeping watch. They each had the tell-tale bulge near their armpit where they carried a gun beneath their jacket. None of them smiled. All of them looked as if they could break Jake in half without working up a sweat.

Gareth sat across the table from Jake and Lauren. He looked very relaxed, calm, and in control. He was also still smiling.

'I'm glad we were able to help,' he said. 'Your deaths would have been a great tragedy. And so unnecessary.'

'You followed us?' asked Jake.

Gareth shook his head.

'Not physically,' he said. 'We followed the signal from your mobile phones; but we'd been listening into your phone conversations, so we already knew where you were headed.'

'How's Robert?' asked Lauren.

'He's fine,' said Gareth. 'A flesh wound, nothing serious. He's being attended to and then we'll send him home, once he's signed the Official Secrets Act.' He looked at Jake. 'You've signed it already, Jake, so I don't think we need to worry about you. But we need your signature, Ms Graham.'

'No,' said Lauren firmly. 'I refuse to keep what's happened hidden.'

Gareth gave a small sigh.

'I thought that might be your attitude,' he said, his tone still smooth and full of charm. 'But I'm sure we can come to some arrangement.'

'I doubt it,' said Lauren curtly.

Gareth smiled.

'We'll come back to that. The main thing is, the book is back in safe keeping.'

'Hidden,' said Lauren. 'The knowledge that it contains denied to people it can help. The greening

248

of the desert! Food from thin air!' She leant forward towards Gareth, visibly angry. 'Can you even imagine the millions of starving people that technology could feed?'

'And can you imagine that technology in the hands of terrorists?' countered Gareth. Now he was no longer smiling. 'That kind of biological weapon could lay waste to a city centre. London. New York. Paris.'

'It could feed the world!'

'It could destroy us,' said Gareth simply.

'Who were they?' asked Jake. It was the question he'd been dying to ask ever since they'd arrived in this room. 'The people who were holding Lauren?'

'We're not yet sure,' said Gareth.

And even if you were, you wouldn't tell me, thought Jake bitterly.

'Pierce Randall?' asked Jake.

Gareth smiled and shook his head. 'Oh no,' he said. 'This was far too crude for a firm like Pierce Randall. They are much more dangerous than that.'

'More dangerous than nearly being shot dead?' demanded Jake.

'There are far worse things than being shot dead,' said Gareth. 'I hope you never have to experience them.' For the first time, Gareth's smile wavered.

He's suffered those worse things, Jake realised with a start. Gareth was a spy of sorts. A very senior spy, but still a spy. And at some time, in his past, Gareth had been there, suffering those terrors that were worse than a quick death by shooting.

'What about the others?' Jake persisted. 'The dead man in my flat.'

'His name was Terry Gibbons,' said Gareth. 'Former SAS. A mercenary. A hit man for hire.'

'Who killed him?'

Gareth smiled. 'Who knows?' he said, his tone enquiringly bland.

You did, thought Jake. You or one of your crowd. 'You did, and then you framed me for it,' he said accusingly.

Gareth looked hurt. 'Jake, how could you accuse me of such a thing?'

'You framed me because you thought it might bring Pierce Randall in.'

'Who is this Pierce Randall?' asked Lauren, puzzled.

It was then that Jake realised he hadn't had the chance to tell her anything about what had happened to him: about the dead man in his flat, or Sue Clark coming to his rescue.

'They're a firm of lawyers,' he replied.

'Oh, they're so much more than that,' said Gareth. 'As I'm sure you must have found out. They have some *very* powerful friends and acquaintances.'

'And you used me as bait to get them in,' challenged Jake.

'They were already in,' replied Gareth smoothly. 'Pierce Randall are a major player in the Malichea business. Possibly *the* major player.'

'I thought the title of the Major Player was held by you,' said Jake. 'The government.'

Gareth shook his head. 'We are just one government,' he said. 'Pierce Randall represents many governments.' Then he added, the tone of his voice changing to a warning, 'And many other organisations as well.'

'Yes,' said Jake. 'I've seen the website.'

'The Watchers showed you, no doubt,' said Gareth.

'The Watchers?' echoed Lauren, even more nonplussed.

'I'll explain them later,' said Jake.

'There's not much to explain,' said Gareth. 'They are basically harmless. Well-meaning, but we do share the same aims.'

'To keep the Malichea books hidden,' said Jake.

'Until the world is ready for them.' Gareth nodded.

'And when will that be?' asked Jake.

Gareth sighed. 'When human nature changes and stops wanting to use new discoveries for the purposes of war and domination, power and greed.'

'In other words, never.'

'That depends whether you are an optimist or a pessimist about humankind,' said Gareth. 'But I think that's enough abstract philosophy. The real question is: what is to be done with you?'

'Why do anything with us?' asked Jake. 'You've got the book. It's over.'

'We both know that isn't the case,' said Gareth. 'Ms Graham has already said she doesn't intend to let this stay hidden. She wants to carry on, searching for the books. And, sooner or later, she may find another one. And the next time we may not be able to do anything about it.' He gave a rueful smile. 'Which does present us with a dilemma. Do we let her remain free to do that, or do we have her locked up for the murder of Carl Parsons?'

'That was self-defence!' burst out Jake hotly.

Lauren looked sadly at Jake. 'I was about to say I didn't do it,' she said in a tired voice.

'Sorry,' mumbled Jake apologetically.

'We listened to your phone conversation,' Gareth reminded them. 'Regardless of what you were about to say, Ms Graham, I'm afraid there is enough evidence pointing to your guilt. Now, it may be true that you could plead self-defence, but really we'd prefer it if you weren't charged at all. If you were charged, there are many things that could come out in court that we'd prefer not to have aired.'

'Like the existence of the books of the Order of Malichea,' said Lauren.

'Exactly.' Gareth nodded. 'At the moment we prefer them to remain as some fantasy. A mythical library believed in by a few harmless crackpots and conspiracy theorists. So, I'm afraid, Ms Graham, you are going to have to die.'

'You can't kill her!' cried Jake, shocked.

Gareth looked at Jake, equally shocked.

'I never suggested killing her,' he said, a pained expression on his face. 'I'm saying that Lauren Graham has to die.' Turning to Lauren he added, 'We will give you a new identity, a background of such perfect creation that no one will ever discover it is false.' He gave a slightly smug smile. 'We are very good at this. We've had to do it on many occasions. However, it will mean you moving to a different country for a while.'

'How long is a while?' asked Lauren, tight-lipped.

'A year or two,' said Gareth. 'Maybe five or ten. It would not be wise for you to return until we tell you that you can.'

'Ten years!' echoed Jake, horrified. He turned to Lauren. He could see the tears in her eyes that she was fighting to hold back.

'You have no family alive except your cousin Robert,' continued Gareth. 'Your parents are dead. There's no one really to ask questions if you disappear.

'I have friends,' said Lauren defiantly.

Gareth shrugged. 'Friends move on,' he said. 'As for Robert, we'll explain the necessity to him.'

Lauren sat silent, and Jake could sense the turmoil that was going on inside her.

Finally, she asked, 'Where are you thinking of sending me?'

'We thought New Zealand,' said Gareth. 'It's a wonderful country.'

'And a long way from England,' said Lauren.

'Yes.' Gareth nodded. 'There is that point as well.'

'And what about me?' asked Jake. 'Do I have to die too?'

'You haven't killed anyone,' said Gareth. 'You can stay here.'

'And if I choose not to?' demanded Jake. 'If I want to go to New Zealand?'

Gareth gave a sad smile.

'I think you might find the authorities in New Zealand may not let you in,' he said. 'They might find your name on a list of terrorist suspects who shouldn't be allowed to enter their country.' He sighed. 'In fact, Jake, I think you might find your name on a list that will make it difficult to leave the country at all.' He turned his attention back to Lauren, then to Jake, and finally addressed them both. 'Well?' he asked. 'What's it to be?'

# Chapter 29

Heathrow Airport. The world's busiest international airport. Hundreds of thousands of passengers flying in and out every day, millions of people seeing them off, saying goodbye to loved ones, or waiting to welcome them as they come through the gates. Arrivals and departures. And right now the international departures area for flights to New Zealand was packed.

They hadn't trusted Lauren not to run. She'd been kept under close guard the whole time since that interview in the basement of the MI6 building, a prisoner. Today was the first time that Jake and Lauren had been able to meet, to talk, without one of MI6's spooks hovering close by. They were still there, but at a discreet distance, watching. Not that Lauren could do much in the way of absconding. The people keeping watch on her had hold of her passport. Or, at least, a passport with her photo inside it and in the name of Samantha

Adams. Her luggage had already gone through and was being loaded on to the Air New Zealand aeroplane.

Jake held Lauren in his arms and hugged her close to him. They stood there, wrapped painfully in one another, like so many hundreds of other couples saying difficult goodbyes.

'I'm sorry,' he said.

'No,' she said. 'If I hadn't brought you into this, none of it would have happened.'

'I phoned you, remember,' said Jake. He sighed. 'Anyway, that wasn't why I was saying sorry. I was saying sorry for being so stupid at that wedding. With . . . whatshername.'

'Alice,' said Lauren.

'Yes,' said Jake. 'With Alice.'

'Not half as stupid as I got with Carl,' said Lauren. She sighed. 'And he only wanted me because he thought he could use me to get to the Malichea books.'

'That's all behind us now,' said Jake. He hugged her close again, and whispered, 'I'm not letting go, you know.'

'You have to,' she said. 'They won't let you on the plane.'

'I mean, searching for the books,' said Jake. 'I'm going to carry on. And, when I find one, I'll let you know.'

'They'll be watching you,' she warned him. 'Your boss. That law firm. That other organisation, the

Watchers. The people who kidnapped me. They'll all be watching you.'

'Not all the time,' said Jake confidently.

'Yes, they will,' said Lauren, worried. 'And next time you may not be so lucky. Next time, you could get killed.'

'No.' Jake shook his head. 'I know what to do now. How to go about it.'

There was a tap on his shoulder. He turned to see an unsmiling woman in a dark suit standing there. Lauren's watcher, her MI6 guardian.

'Time to go,' said the woman to Lauren. 'We're going to get you on board before the rush.'

'One minute,' begged Lauren.

The woman hesitated, then nodded. 'One minute,' she agreed.

Lauren turned back to Jake.

'They haven't said we can't be in touch. We can phone one another. Skype,' she said.

'They'll try,' said Jake. 'But whatever they try, we'll get round it. They won't keep us apart.'

Lauren looked up into his face.

'I love you, Jake,' she said softly, and suddenly she began to cry silently, tears rolling down her face. 'I never stopped. That's why what you did that day hurt me so much. When I saw you again outside the British Library, I realised my feelings were still as strong as ever.'

'Why didn't you say something?' he begged. 'I haven't ever stopped thinking about you and loving you. And these last few days, since I saw you again . . .'

'I know,' said Lauren. 'But . . . I didn't know if I could trust you again. And, I suppose, part of me wanted you to be jealous about Carl, to feel hurt like I'd been hurt.'

'I did feel jealous,' admitted Jake. 'I hated him because he had you.'

'He didn't have me,' said Lauren. 'Not really. I was always yours.'

'And I'll always be yours,' said Jake.

'You have to go,' interrupted the woman, her voice harder now. 'Otherwise I'll be forced to call security.'

'No,' said Lauren. She released her arms from around Jake and stepped back. 'I love you, Jake,' she said. 'I always will.'

'I love you, Lauren,' said Jake. And now he could feel his own tears running unashamedly down his face. He stepped forward and grabbed her in his arms for one last kiss.

Then she had broken away from him and was heading towards the gate, the MI6 woman walking close beside her. At the gate Lauren turned, and waved, and blew him a kiss, and then went through and was lost in the crowds.

Jake stood, watching the gate, hoping against hope

that things would change, that she'd return, that Gareth would change his mind, that she'd walk back through to him and fling her arms around him and they'd run off into the sunset to spend their lives together. But she never came.

After an hour, when the flight had been called, and the board announced that it had departed, only then did Jake turn and head for the exit.

Yes, she'd gone. But the planet was small. He'd see her again. And next time, he'd have something special for her. A book. One of the Malichea books.

'Next time,' thought Jake determinedly. 'Next time . . .'

Want to know what happens next?
Read on for a gripping taster of
THE DEADLY GAME . . .

# Prologue

The screams came from the man tied to the chair in the middle of the room. He'd been screaming for hours, in between sobbing and pleading for the torture to stop. There were two other men in the room. One was tall and muscular, with the broken nose of a boxer. The other, small and wiry, was holding something metal in his hand that glistened with blood. Both men looked on impassively, although the shorter man's face seemed to show a hint of a smile. The man in the chair suddenly slumped forward, his blood-soaked body straining against the ropes that held him. Boxer frowned and ran his fingers down the side of the tortured man's neck, feeling for a pulse. Then he switched to the wrist, the tips of his fingers searching for a sign of life beneath the flayed skin of the man's arm.

He looked up and shook his head. 'He's dead,' he said.

The short man scowled. Just then his mobile phone rang. He pressed the phone to his ear, and then said abruptly: 'No, he ain't talked.' He cast a look of annoyance at the body strapped in the chair and added: 'And he ain't likely to any more.'

He listened some more, then hung up. He turned to Boxer. 'He says forget about him. He's got another job for us.'

Boxer gestured towards the lifeless body. 'What about him?' he asked.

The short man gave an evil grin.

'One for the pigs,' he said.

# Chapter 1

Jake Wells sat in front of his computer and smiled into his webcam, beaming at the face looking back at him from his screen. Lauren Graham. Fugitive, exile, killer; his girlfriend.

He looked at the clock. 11 p.m. here in the UK. 11 a.m. in Wellington, New Zealand. In the old days people had to content themselves with intercontinental phone calls and echoing time delays. But now, with Skype, they could see one another, even though they were on opposite sides of the globe.

It was three months ago that Lauren had boarded a plane for New Zealand to start a new life with a new identity. Samantha Adams. That was what it said on her passport, her birth certificate and all the other documents MI5 had provided for her. But to Jake, she would always be Lauren.

'I went on a trip to South Island the other week,' she

said. 'We went to the Franz Josef Glacier. It's amazing. It runs down to rainforest – two totally contrasting climates right next to each other . . .'

'We?' Jake said, his heart sinking. Had she met someone else?

Lauren laughed.

'Me and a girl from work,' she reassured him, sensing his discomfort. 'She's really nice. Her name's Anna. She works with me at the research centre.'

The Antarctic Survey Research Centre, where Lauren – or rather, Sam Adams – had found a job studying environmental information from the base stations all over Antarctica.

Jake smiled.

'I've been doing some exploring, too,' he told her. 'Last week I went for a stroll at a place called Firle Beacon . . .'

There was a pinging sound from the screen, and suddenly the image of Lauren vanished. In its place a message appeared: *An error has occurred. This programme will close.*

And then, as Jake watched, one by one the logos on the screen disappeared and finally the screen went blank. His computer had shut down.

He pressed the keys to reboot it. While it was starting up, he picked up his landline phone and dialled Lauren's mobile number. He got an automated message telling him: 'The mobile you are calling is unavailable. Please try later.'

He cursed. Lauren's mobile wasn't switched off. They'd been cut off, deliberately. It had happened a lot when she had first been in New Zealand, but they'd learned that it was always when they started talking about Malichea and the hidden books. So they'd been more careful, and for quite a while they'd only discussed day-to-day things, where they'd been, what movies they'd seen.

Sometimes he'd be silly and romantic, holding up a single red rose towards the camera and then feeling happiness pour through him as she told him how much she wished they could be together again.

'We will be,' he promised her.

He didn't know how, there were so many obstacles to overcome, but he knew they were destined to be together. He needed her properly in his life – not just a moving image of her on a computer screen.

He tried phoning her again, but the connection was still broken.

He sighed and sent her an email, and hoped they'd at least allow this through to her . . .